FICTION

WWW.INDEPENDENTLEGIONS.COM

MULTIPLE BRAM STOKER AWARD WINNER

ALESSANDRO MANZETTI

THE KEEPER OF CHERNOBYL

NOVELLA

ISBN: 979-12-80713-64-3
JULY 2023

ORIGINALLY PUBLISHED IN 2019 BY OMNIUM GATHERUM
TRANSLATED BY DANIELE BONFANTI
EDITED BY LEE MURRAY

2019 BRAM STOKER AWARD NOMINATED
SUPERIOR ACHIEVEMENT IN LONG FICTION

RECIPIENT OF HWA SPECIALTY PRESS AWARD

THE KEEPER OF CHERNOBYL

TABLE OF CONTENTS

For Maja, my little undying dawn.

MULTIPLE BRAM STOKER AWARD WINNER

ALESSANDRO MANZETTI

THE KEEPER OF CHERNOBYL

Prometheus Returns

To Boni, my white peach

June 22, 1964
Semipalatinsk Military Base Balapan
Bunker 117

What I'm about to write in here won't end up on the steel shelves of an armored warehouse, or inside the stone belly of some secret military base a few meters from the Ark of the Covenant or the Führer's scorched skull.

This isn't to be taken too seriously, it's nothing of scientific value; just a journal, where I'll scribble whatever comes to mind. I don't even know why I'm staining these off-white pages with ink. Perhaps, it's simply because I'm lonely; or so I might hide somewhere—maybe under the bed—a black box of my thoughts, the musings of a guinea pig with a tendency for poetry and madness.

I won't record riverside strolls, nor Henry Miller's Paris sidewalks; I won't draw any face, real or imagined, and I won't stuff it with cheap poems and stories either.

I'm a scientist. My life has become subterranean lately, so—claustrophobically—the core of my narrative is a project, my final one, which is swallowing me whole. It's something that doesn't exist, shouldn't exist, but in these underground tunnels it has a codename nonetheless: Prometheus.

No, it's not an urban legend. There are hundreds of us down here, in the Balapan Bunker, and if anyone has already told this story...well, they weren't that crazy.

But they were certainly good in making themselves scarce.

We live in these tunnels like worms in white coats, breast-feeding our litter of atomic soldiers, those who'll rule on the battlefield; we're preparing them, transforming 12 Prometheus Returns them to this very end. No romance, no science fiction. *Realpolitik.*

I'm not raving, of that much I'm sure... I've got hard data about my mental health, papers full of the right numbers: here, everybody is under constant medical control.

No time to waste, is what they told us, even before setting the labs up. When Earth is overturned by the Green Apocalypse—the mushroom-headed God Plutonium— and becomes something very different, you'll have to pick sides: either among the masters of the surface, or the earthworms, below, sheltered, without sun, their eyes shrinking, turning small like a needle's to adjust to the new environment.

The Soviet Way to address this new, post-apocalyptic world—of which I'm but a small cog—will be to recolonize this future Earth-2 with its lethal gamma rays for rainbows (just slightly cozier than Mars). *What does that mean?* We'll want to stay topside, for sure, and to make that possible we're working two hundred meters underground.

The idea is simple: creating a small genetically-modified army, with blue skin and silver gaze, fit to survive to the extremes of a thermonuclear war already taking its first steps—red buttons already pressed on both sides—while we, still-standard humans with a red star on our chests, will stay down here for five or six years, waiting for military control of the war zones. Eventually, we'll be able to apply the mutation wholesale, like a vaccine. We'll rise from our underground hives, like this bunker, as a new species.

Our generals are already daydreaming, easy prey to visions of Armageddon and paybacks. The red flag flapping on a gutted Pentagon, surrounded by a mountain of vitrified ants, and an even bigger ant with a still-lit Cuban cigar in its mouth. The fat workers of a Ford factory in their antiradiation outfits, a wide-faced Uncle Sam whose lost all his hair printed on the back, everybody hard at work to tame the machines of a new mass-production line: millions of single-dose cans, synthetic proteins for their galleries of screaming survivors.

The military always makes things simple. There's so much more going on: most of all, we must think about the aftermath, about an Earth-2 actually works. And when the future has to be re-engineered, that's where we enter my favorite field. Since childhood, I've always imagined the tail of things… I'm not talking about lizards, or sadistic teenage experiments: I mean the actual future, the *final* tail of things.

That's the reason I became a scientist. To flush out the impossible, pinch the little demon who's always a millimeter away—and yet just there, before your eyes—who's able to let the cat out of the bag and turn research into fact, into true change.

That elusive critter has a short tail. It's hard to catch; clever, it hides well behind the geometric stiffness of reality and old theories. You have to leave a trail of breadcrumbs in the right places to lure it in. More than anything, you need to believe that impossibilities really do exist.

I'm a pragmatist, of course, that's my job. Nor am I a dreamer, but I approach to everything with that essential ingredient discovered in my youth: a sense of wonder toward small things, how they work, and how they suddenly change. What you take for granted, what you ignore because it's banal, has always been my polar star, my direction. Like a water diviner, I chased those vibrations, those intuitions, running back and forth, studying phenomena, and becoming ever more invested in genetics—a field that, more than any other, explains and transforms reality. Human reality, the most complex and fascinating of all.

In my personal life, this innate rhabdomancy never worked nearly as well: in life, you don't need spinning DNA helices, but solid bricks to pile up, and you'd better look at closer stars; but that's another story and someday maybe I'll get to it. If I have enough pages.

So we're at hard at it, working to assure Soviet topside survival, but it'll be some time before we're ready to field-test and deploy our first platoon of next-gen soldiers, unleashing them on future battlefields. Although, who knows? We may need them tomorrow morning. All it takes is a Yankee index finger pressing the wrong button…

It will take weeks, months of analyses, checks, and tests before we're truly ready. Turning points need time, as any transition from the old requires time to spark anew. If we're lucky, if our politicians and bureaucrats manage to shuffle the decks and gain time, we'll be ready when the alarms flash, and things get busy up there…missiles painted in kitsch blue or nice Soviet red, curving in space, getting cold, bearing down on targets *zero, one, two, three.* And then, turning on everything else that exists on the surface, up to target *five thousand and one.*

Down here, in the Bunker, with our neon sun and the bitter taste of ammonia in our mouth from sucked-and-recycled oxygen, we're all together—fathers and sons of manipulated genetic branches. Ours is a weird factory of limited editions…

I had to hide the journal under a heap of stats when a security henchman blew into the lab, perhaps picking up the scent of a very special truffle: around here even an iota of proof of sabotage is worth a medal and a class-B flat.

Inspection, Professor Pavlov! Code 11. They're all like that: glossy-eyed, dilated pupils, codes to be repeated, procedures. The immortal breed of human parrots armed with AK-47s. Golden buttons, oversized jackets, a flying saucer on their heads.

I gratified him with an extra dose of adrenaline: he can certainly use that to drag the *abortions* down to the Floor -7 cages; they're are worse than a jealous Siberian woman, they scratch… and bite, mostly.

Abortions. That's what they call subjects who reject the treatment, and they're becoming a real issue. You could say we forge monsters, sometimes, just like combinations of X and Y chromosomes shape people, or series of 0's and 1's turn a circuit into an action.

But I prefer the term *rejections* for these genetic errors: it's more accurate, and it helps to maintain a degree of detachment from the allegories which are likely to arise in a place like this; it's an easy step from advanced genetic experimentation facility to horror zoo. Words matter; they change thoughts, and those change all the rest.

But maybe we should talk about *monsters* full-stop: the over-seasoned soup of scientific staff buried down here, including the two-bit colleagues, as slimy salamanders, so cunning that they managed to get assigned to a project like this despite their lack of competence. These particular gentlemen couldn't light a match by themselves, let alone steal fire from gods…like the old-school, obsolete Prometheus.

So, here we are: monsters and their step-masters.

Now that I've spring-charged the rejection tamer with adrenaline, doing what I'm doing right under his nose— industrial espionage, and against myself!—I won't be disturbed until the next inspection. Three hours, more or less, without having to smell the fresh-paint odor of KGB puppets; they'll take another swing after dinner, as always—to ruin your digestion. And not once, have they brought dessert. Which means I've got plenty of time to jot down some lines about my atomic spawn, my champions.

Konstantin, a big red-headed youth, came to the Bunker two years ago. He's from Zhalanash, where he spent his first, crisp twenty years, fishing with his father on the Aral. They were both already doomed, in need of a new livelihood, considering their lake—hunting ground where so many hopes floated—is about to evaporate and turn into a swamp, only good to grow rice.

Lake, what a nice word for something that will soon look like a huge pan left on the fire, the squat crafts abandoned there, dark brown and caked with salt. *Thanks to the Kremlin's intensive farming plan.*

Konstantin was among the first to be treated. *Increase the flow, Professor*, I can take it. So proud, the big boy, with bright eyes that stared at things, that gaze of guys like 16 Prometheus Returns him, young people with a straight back and hands cooked by hard work—but quick to lose their heads a draw a knife in a card game. Survival warriors.

People accustomed to making do, without letting a single crumb drop. *No lake or fish? Good, let's move to plan B. That evaporates as well? You still have the rest of the alphabet.* In short, that's how his brain works.

My champion never wore a watch, and neither did he try to conceive any life plan, let alone a smug one. Make do. So long as it's bread and butter. Something in his childhood must have vaccinated him against having high expectations. Not a bad thing, after all, for someone like him, with precious little in the way of opportunity, and the unseen words "slave" and "poor" branded behind his ears. Tune in on a stable wavelength, a simple one, without too many voices or dials; wake up with the sun from Monday to Saturday; and think about bringing home your net full of stuff to eat.

And what about Sunday? Well, for Sundays there was Marina. A female all flesh and French cigarettes—or so he told me that time, boasting.

All true, of course: in villages like Zhalanash, you just need a few rubles and a short bicycle ride to rent love and satisfy other silent urges. The salt of resilience.

Since Day One, the big lake boy presented himself as the perfect subject, with a high ability to adapt. It's one of the main non-biological traits we seek in our candidates.

He never disappointed me and has always risen to the occasion, exceeding any expectation. With those strong fingers, marked by a sailor's knots, he clenched his fists during the treatment in the immersion pools, while all the other specimens cried like ambulances as their bones were burning like torches.

The first month of experimentation was the hardest. Here, in the Bunker, my chemist colleagues (they liked them thin and bearded, as though looking an Arabalchemist could be an asset) were tasked with preparing the proto-liquid we use for sustained exposition, wasting dozens of candidates before coming up with the right proportions of vector-enzymes and K liquid plutonium.

Of course, it was the first time something like this had even been tried... Still, experiments might have been conducted without necessarily melting the bulk of the human material. *Butchers. But better to say that in a whisper, or to write it in small letters.*

We're in a secret base, and it would be all too easy to end up into the same simmering cauldron as those poor devils. When you're in a place like this, you look straight ahead, following the yellow track they paint in front of you. You can't afford to show sympathy and, unfortunately, you get used to pretending that you haven't seen a thing.

There is no point going into the science in a journal. I'll gladly spare myself the two hundred pages that would be necessary to trace the basic boundaries of Project Prometheus. Half my day is already slave to that secret-archive, since all my research (and that of my team) is thoroughly recorded as it is, then put under lock and key every night.

The Bunker is full of vampires—not only monsters and butchers. They're balled up and sleeping under steel girders. The bloodsuckers store the products of our brains, dropping ice cubes onto the fresh-squeezed juices of our insights and they guard them, counting every single step forward. Bureaucratic creatures with sharp features, ink and blood in their veins, they sleep through the day to feed on what we've developed in our worktime. Creatures (human ones) against whom holy water and ash stakes are a waste of time.

Have you delivered today's report, Professor? They seem kind, those guys, but you must not trust them. Professor Termikanov could tell you something about that, if they hadn't forced him to swallow tens of liters of water, until he burst. It can happen. A spy—real or alleged—is worth a medal and a class-B flat. Shiny things.

So, I'm not in the mood to explain what we do here, in the Prometheus unit. A few words are more than enough, as far as I'm concerned, considering they're not intended for me, but for whoever might one day find this journal.

We're talking post-eugenics; recombination and gene therapy, *a new bright Sparta, glittering like Vega in the pitch black of traditional science.* I'm just mocking propaganda. It's a free territory, and I'll do what I like. Writing is therapy, after all.

No mega-freezers full of embryos, cell jams, mysterious bacterial cultures or anything of the sort: in the Bunker, that doesn't exist. We work on already existing, naturally-grown material; that's the beauty of it. We just add—in the right way, following standard procedures—the secret ingredient, the glue of Earth-2: *plutonium, in all its possible oxidations.* No surprise about that: Hiroshima and Nagasaki opened the barn door, and the atomic cows are long since loose.

How's our crazy scheme going? *Did we come up with the recipe for radioactive Coca Cola?* Are we ready to take over the world when the Green Apocalypse occurs? *Has Prometheus been resurrected?* We're working on that, but our hero isn't ready to rise yet. Something went wrong and our timeline stretched. Until three months ago, things were running smoothly, but then the abortions began. Same old problem. A degenerative curve was expected, but we certainly didn't expect to be facing a *genetic plague*—let alone one serious as the one we're experiencing now. It doesn't affect my chosen ones, the subjects entrusted to my team: Konstantin and Boni (I haven't introduced her yet, because she's like dessert and must come at the end). But the other specimens, those in the care of my colleagues, have been affected, despite all the research teams following the same treatment protocol for their subjects. And yet results are different and more often than is understandable. Monsters and chosen ones, everything or nothing. A whole factory of outcasts alongside the successful one. *What's the problem, what's making the difference?*

Is it just a matter of time, perhaps, before we see the wraith of rejection strike all subjects? Will they all turn into monsters? That's exactly what we must discover, before moving to wider scale production.

Konstantin is among the three hundred subjects who've reached Level 3. Next week, we'll start working on lipid transfers and central grafts. On his brain… delicate stuff. His heart can already pump *green nourishment* by itself without breaking apart, so our goal is close. The big boy will make it, I'm sure. He'll bring home the bacon again, somehow.

And then, there's Boni, the apple of my eye, my other chosen one. Things with her are different, and I confess my approach, in her case, isn't merely technical or scientific. I can write it: here, it doesn't matter.

The trap was obvious, and it sprang virtually straight away: many scientists are so committed to their research (a life's research) that they feel an ardor beyond love—an ever-overvalued emotion. The same is true for me, but the difference is that my project is a person, Boni; a girl from Kiev, who could make you rip your heart from your chest. A young woman destined to become a new Eve, maybe the first of her species, if things go as they must.

I never imagined anything like that back in my student days, when I was busy polishing the shoes of some Lomonosov windbag, before they built the Vorob'ëvy Gory campus, and the highest tower in the world…well, not counting the filthy scrapers of New York.

Loneliness was the trigger (bait?) of the trap. I'm not afraid of writing that, nor to confess it, considering I'm confessing to myself: I need that girl to bear life…or at least, what life has become. Because many things have changed, and too quickly. And Prometheus and the future Earth-2 have nothing to do with that.

Words can't describe what Boni really is for me… she's many, too many things overlapping, confusing me, stunning me, flinging me on cloud nine and then so low, just an instant later, that my feet are scorched at the core of the Earth. For me, that girl is a multiform virus. She can take on a number of appearances: lost youth, resurrected daughter, a new radioactive bride (maybe, one day…), intuition in flesh and bone—and many other things that elude me.

During the first phase of treatment—the most painful—I heard Boni screaming, laughing, crying, surviving and dying, promising anything a man desires to make the flow stop… that never-ending burn, because I was the one controlling the machines. I was the searing sun, and I could not get clouded—not even for a second.

Yes, *those damned pools for proto-liquid immersion*, boiling transformations that made the skin feel as it were tearing away from the bone. And sometimes it actually happened.

A necessary step for all candidates. A torture even for us, behind the psychedelic keyboard of pain. There's no other way.

From day one, I loved that girl with the eyes of an old god licking his lips on the other side of the galaxy. Whose desires, of course, are the same as any normal man with basic drives; but who knows when it's time to cool to boiling rain of Venus.

Boni came here very young, sixteen years old, a white peach dropping on your shoulder when you're already thinking that your season has come and gone. And then becoming your only lifeline some months later, when you're thinking about giving up, topping yourself (if only you could just stop breathing, sometimes), when Madame Depression runs around you with her quick little legs, raising a large oval mirror to reflect your greatest failing. Lada, my daughter, in Pool 1, a summer Tuesday when they were still setting up the labs and the equipment of the hard-experimentation areas, and all the human material, including Boni, was stocked on Floor -4, going through the never-ending preliminary tests. *Convulsions, blood from her mouth, emerald green, glowing.*

She wasn't ready, nothing really was, back then.

And yet I wanted to be the first to make it. *For a simple medal? For an A-class flat, close to Lomonosov?*

Of course not; I did it because I wanted my daughter to be the first post-atomic woman. I envisaged her as Botticelli's Venus, with her hair of grain, rising from a stillalive Ural and blessing the craters of nuclear explosions from her plutonium-plated seashell. But…*convulsions, blood from her mouth, emerald green, glowing.* That's what happened, leaving behind a black hole screaming with emptiness, to be filled no matter what.

The tasks of forging a next-gen Amazon, able to ride phosphorescent steppes and breathe gamma rays, and putting together a new daughter, fused into one, letting time confound me with their overlapping faces… She looks so much like her. Maybe she'll be the one forgiving me, someday. The one alive.

That's Boni for me. Biting into the blue apple of the future, while the present snaps between my fingers, and the hypnotic voodoo of wait beats its drums.

AUGUST 2, 1964
SEMIPALATINSK MILITARY BASE BALAPAN
BUNKER 117

It's hot as hell, today. They say the air conditioning has broken down, even if the pumps keep us breathing, here underground, wheezing like worms with disproportioned lungs.

They do that to punish us; they want to make us suffer, to sweat our thoughts out, because of delays in the project. Like it's a walk in the park, creating a new breed of radioactive Spartans… You can't just reach out and brush the fingertip of the new Adam, like Michelangelo imagined. Or the nipples of a new Eve with glowing breasts. You can't just transfer the 'Prometheus' code into them in a single, demiurgic second.

Explain that to the bureaucrats as they eat up mountains of papers like goats. But in fact, not every team is in a hurry to completing all the phases of the program, and field-test the first specimens—several are moving at a snail's pace…

There are reasons. Fear and anguish: better to endure the heat, our inspectors' foul breath, and make it through the winter inside the steel belly of this bunker, than to end up like varnish for the Kremlin domes. As soon as we're finished with our work, and our research is all on record, rumor has it that they'll use our vitrified skin for tiles.

Secrecy; a nasty word, bleeding all too often around here… Everywhere, in this facility—doors, papers, tags— we read the words TOP SECRET, and they look ever larger. It's all true: it's dangerous to work on projects like this, fear is justified.

But there's another problem. When you spend too much time in isolation—that's what happens in a bunker— you risk going insane, and all it takes is a fixation to begin whirling in your head to fry your brain.

Initially, we could call home every day and visit our families once a month; but then security became tighter and tighter. Now…two phone calls a month is all they allow us, to make us feel part of the world out there. Not much. But you have to make the best of it.

Yesterday, I took the opportunity to call old Orazm, my favorite smuggler of good (though not very patriotic) music.

He made me listen to three minutes from the future: *A Hard Day's Night* by the Beatles. If he keeps transmitting that stuff through government lines, sooner or later they'll slit his throat like a pig. The Beatles—the Western virus— the vitriolic new strain, able to knock Brežnev's from his dias.

Then, that song still on my mind, I phoned Klara— Lada's mother. I'm a masochist of the worst kind, I cannot do without having her poisonous stinger driven into my side. My lady, or what's left of her after my daughter's funeral—*a box, my child in a fucking shoe box!*—did not miss her chance, squeezing the trigger like a well-trained sniper. Blood calling for more blood: *You worm, why don't you go for a swim in your nice pools, get picked clean to the marrow, instead of bugging me with your whining?* Isolation is best, sometimes.

But it no longer matters, I'm numb to that venom, as I risk becoming numb to everything else were it not for Boni breathing inside me like a soft demon, keeping me alive. Luckily, I must look after her for sixteen hours a day. Such is my generous dose of daily oxygen.

Her new blue pigmentation—the epidermal variation the subjects show after about ten sessions of nucleo-dialysis—really suits her: she's beautiful. We've just completed the tests to confirm her ascent to Level 3, like Konstantin.

It was hard. I was afraid of losing her. Her eyes are constantly open. Watery, they stare at the ceiling; but soon, her gaze will be even more alive and pure, with her sockets deep in the shiny silver of K liquid plutonium. No more darkness for her. From now on, no more night, only stars.

My atomic Amazon will be able to run and fight even if the sun goes dark. She'll mock Lady Electricity when she lifts her skirt to a new Iron Age, all black and with no fires in sight. To an age of boundless post-atomic deserts, ribbed with the stumps of missiles, and the mutilated, blackened sculptures of what used to be human, alive, and evolved.

Today, Konstantin asked me when he's going to be field-tested; he feels ready.

For the last two weeks, I haven't been able to get close to him: he's in the stress chamber, where he's enduring a bombardment of high-frequency gamma rays (by now, for him, it's like hugging a second, electromagnetic mother).

I can watch his resilience through the wide window of the control room, as thick as the supporting wall of an old house. I'm alone, and I can write what I'm seeing for once, without having to rely on my memory.

The color of the youth's skin varies from Prussian blue to azure; a phenomenon observed only in the last few days. An interesting interaction. We talk through a croaking intercom. His appearance is still human, but K plutonium runs through his veins, greasing the helices of his mutated DNA, slowly turning him into something different. A hairless Spartacus of the XX century, with quivering enhanced muscles, an elongated skull, gills on both sides of his neck, and his toes beginning to withdraw as they face the stressors of evolution. His mouth has been cleared of those useless ivory appendages; you no longer need teeth if you can suck the green nectar of the Cold War, a radioactive, lethal cocktail that his new biological configuration can enjoy like fresh orange juice.

This happens in the stress chamber, and it's just the beginning.

Only three days ago, he still looked more or less like a normal young man, though the bomb of change was already primed inside him. If he survives—if he walks out of the stress chamber on his two legs—we'll be able to assess him at Level 4. We're so close to our final goal, I can't believe it.

So, he's still alive inside there, and all I can do is watch as he becomes the future he always kept at a distance, a future he couldn't even imagine, there in his small village, with an old wood stove that had to keep ten people warm.

He gets up, approaches, clenches his jaw and gestures to me that he wants out, pointing at the armored door. It's not time yet. I shake my head and he gets angry, beating his fists against the pane of his atomic fish tank. *Resist, my prince.* He can still make out my outline, the shadow of the sorcerer who stuffed him with that weird, silvery magic— but he's going slowly blind. As expected, no abortions with me. We'll have to graft a visor on him, linked to his optic nerve, but there's time for that.

Today, Boris—one of Professor Kireyev's candidates— will undergo the stress chamber, too. It's a mistake, and that bastard's team (he's a real butcher) well knows that, but they're playing dumb. *He's a man who can call the Kremlin even at night.* That's the urban legend going around down here, and he certainly takes every advantage of it.

His boy isn't ready. Boris was just assessed at Level 3, and hastily—they didn't even put him through the tests Boni is currently passing. But I'm not one for racing, putting my specimens' skin on the line.

Right, Boni. My white peach. She's always intruding on my thoughts; a few lines, and she always reappears.

SEPTEMBER 25, 1964
SEMIPALATINSK MILITARY BASE
FIELD-TEST PERIMETER

He killed them all, a real war machine.

They let Konstantin loose on the surface for the fieldtest and he reacted as expected within this action perimeter surrounded by ionizing fans. In short, a big raw, fighting ring with forced radioactivity. Ten men, dressed as soldiers and well-armed and with basic protection; Kazak cannon fodder (they had loaded them up on a truck by force, at the village of Iaksha) and turned into makeshift elite corps. *Living targets.* All too easy, for a subject like my boy, by now as fast as a rocket and tough as an icebreaker.

Not a pretty sight, the one I shared with General Semerov from watchtower 17, overlooking this immense, jagged atomic polygon that can simulate Earth-2 better than anything else in the world.

The General—arrived from Kurtschatow at dawn, out of breath and with his nose still stained with milk— drooled marvel onto his oversized gray coat. He must have felt like King of the Slaughterhouse, crowned as he was by the Ural Mountains jutting sharply behind his shoulders. At the end of the simulation, he ran out like a plump kid after his ball. Dressed like a deep-sea diver, squeezed inside his antiradiation outfit, he stopped in his tracks on the bloodied steppe, his arms spread like a holy man receiving some divine grace. He was already calculating on the emperor-like dacha he'd just earned himself, wedged in the woods with the peaks of the Caucasus at a hand's reach, close enough to use them as spicy pork skewers for his guests. A toast among medals and whores. *The war will be won!*

But those were corpses, under his boots...he almost tripped on souls, two-by-two, craning their necks, waiting to be sucked up into that gray sky of nothingness. The shapes scattered on the ground were the livid bodies of fishermen just like Konstantin, experts in the currents and eddies of the Irtyš which had fed them for so many years.

Yes. That's what was dished up to the villages and towns too close to our base, the land crossed by contaminated rivers, and the wells sucking on tainted aquifers: they were fed perches and carps with glowing scales and spiced with upturned neutrons, ready to be cooked and stick cancer into your bones.

Professor Pavlov! Professor! screamed the General from out there, forcing me from my post, where I was prompted to move by some not-so-kind shoves from a couple of his Siberian goons, their mustaches still frozen.

Konstantin had really killed them all, those poor devils, and with his bare hands. He hadn't even bothered to snatch an assault rifle from the hands of that slapdash brigade, to use it against them. His arms and legs are so strong that he could pierce their bodies, reaching their internal organs.

It went down just as it was supposed to—though I was expecting a more professional field-test; and most certainly not one requiring the sacrifice of a group of fishermen. It wasn't necessary. But the project protocol doesn't require that the scientific staff know the time lines and modality of any field-tests.

My candidate went beyond the requirements to consider his field-test successful: he smashed those poor devils' bodies just like he'd twisted—with no apparent effort—the still-smoking barrels of the old AK-47s tied to the fishermen's arms. Right: our targets needed to be armed; ready to open fire, not flee. They certainly weren't informed that they'd be spraying blanks (I discovered later); since damaging a specimen like Konstantin would be too much of a waste. A fix of adrenaline instilled short-lived courage into the veins of our wretched platoon. Facing the rough sneer of a sturgeon is no doubt different from the foe they faced this morning. The blue-skinned atomic soldier who, before attacking as instructed, puffed up his neck and rattled his hardly-human gills, then tilted his elongated head on either side, like a boxer getting up from his corner for the first round—a few vertebrae threateningly creaking.

Well, I must say…for a moment—despite the waste of human lives—I felt proud; like a father noticing the first signs of a beard sprouting on his son's face. Konstantin was growing up. A twentieth century Hercules, the Prometheus we were trying to resurrect from the genomes of ordinary mortals who can barely write their name.

Professor Pavlov! And so! The General kept gesticulating, staring at me with disbelieving eyes, as large as tennis balls.

I'm leaving for Moscow immediately. This is some news! I congratulate all your team. So he said, though it was only the first field-test...nothing final, not yet. But the Kremlin is eager to get a positive update about the project, after so many drawbacks and failures, causing our total isolation in the belly of the Bunker; but I've already written about that. *Two phone calls a month,* until we see some results.

Easy for the military to say. Modifying human genes isn't the same as pinning a medal on your chest because you watched through a telescope—from a position of safety, a smooth Cuban cigar in your mouth—a new model of tank crashing through a few dozens of rebels armed with slingshots. But that's how it's worked, since forever.

The truth is that Konstantin, besides the poor fishermen's attack, survived yet another radioactive bombardment, and with no gear. But we still have a lot of work to do, and the subjects being treated by my worn-out colleagues are lagging behind—let alone the abortions shut in the guts of our labyrinth of underground tunnels. *Fearful cries, day and night.*

Boni screamed, too, and at length, while absorbing the effects of the Level 3 bursts. Seventy-two hours of geometric delirium. But her condition seems good now; she's calm, and all our analyses offer comforting data. Before we can set her first field-test, though...she'll have to endure the stress chamber.

The human body certainly wasn't made to assimilate liquid plutonium, not even little by little. I don't think the Creator, despite his infinite wisdom, could imagine a total nuclear war while modeling Adam; let alone the need for land forces capable of surviving the most hostile environment. He couldn't have thought about the Green Apocalypse, otherwise he too would have used liquid plutonium and K phases, armoring his Adam, the first Prometheus, for the darker days.

OCTOBER 12,
1964 MOSCOW – CAFÉ PUSHKIN

No underground and no bunker for today.

General Semerov may be an absurd character, but his report—the one he delivered to Moscow in his teeth— worked: they loosened our leashes. Thanks to Konstantin's positive field-test, and Kireyev's cynicism—nullingevery every security protocol, that butcher managed to assess his Boris at Level 4—we've been freed from the isolation of the base, and now we're enjoying a short leave. Fresh air. Eighteen hours, not even twenty-four; but I've given up trying to understand the logic of our alabaster-headed supervisors.

And now, unusually cheerful, I'm leaning my belly against one of the crooked tables at Café Pushkin, Moscow, emptying my third glass of vodka.

Klara was here with me until a few minutes ago, on a now-empty chair. *Look at you, worm, you're miserable.* By seeing her again in person, I was hoping her dark eyes might regard me again like they used to, back when we were both students at Lomonosov, when she made me feel like the champion of the male race, an imaginary laurel-wreath covering the baldness already irking me. I asked her to marry me in this exact place, in my awkward manner, throwing a hot coffeepot at her and then—still unsatisfied—letting her pay the bill. I'd left my wallet and documents back at the university, in my first office as assistant (a hole), where I worked under the vigilant eye of comrade Stalin in his frame on the wall. He would defend them.

I couldn't do anything right, but back then I still had the pass-card of love, which forgives everything; and walking with my bizarre gait—an odd, almost hopping beat that even today makes people grin—I felt my wings grow, ready to land on heaven. The

Hyperuranion of Moscow was at a hand, and I would taste its approach, daily, for five years.

Comrade Pavlov, you're a lucky bastard. How many times did I hear that? Or the other one, the shortest endearment of them all—*I love you*, whispered through bedsheets, a warm breeze of conspiracy and complicity, as we would shut ourselves off from the world with all its useless contraptions.

I was overcome with happiness, my life flooded with light.

Lada was born, my daughter. Since that day, since the first smile animated by that small, vulnerable body well-determined to survive even inside her incubator, I emerged from the frozen wasteland of my life.

But today, apparently, everything has changed; that wasteland—melancholy, loneliness—reclaimed its icy territory inside me.

It has invaded me.

Lada screams in those cursed pools. Every night she screams in my head, where she left the last memory of her existence—in my arms and in those, so much firmer and less loving, of liquid plutonium.

That's why Klara is so hell-bent on crushing me like vermin. She wants me dead, and she's right. *This is no longer a place for you…worm, get back underground, and stay there.* She vanished with these words, together with the invisible cloud of her pervasive perfume. My hands are bloodied up to my wrists: who knows if others notice, besides her.

It's very cold outside, but the fireplace here does its job, and the wooden bookcases soak in heat like generous braziers. Vodka, too, little by little, is playing its part. Just as expected, no more.

I've brought the journal with me: for once, I liked the idea of scribbling my thoughts in it, outside the roaring environment of the lab, far away from my small room in the Bunker—that wouldn't be fitting for a waitress. And yet they tell me sleeping alone is a privilege. And it's true: many scientists, especially young ones, are heaped in ten-bed dormitories. Though, you still have only one bathroom for each accommodation area (nothing worse than a communist bunker, in this case), and by night, when the restrooms in the experimentation area cannot be used, the line is always long.

It would be better to forget work, at least for the next twelve hours, and think about something else. But I keep bringing Boni up in my head…no way to avoid it, not even in this café with its annoying chatter washing over you. What might she be doing now? I saw her this morning, before leaving the base and hopping on the helicopter— courtesy of the Red Army. *Russian intelligentsia in flight, a brain squadron.*

The girl from Kiev was painting something with her fingers on the steel walls of her cell. But then she turned and covered her work with her body, sticking out her tongue at me. I could just glimpse the red and blue lines, which seemed to trace humanlike figures.

Where did she find colors in there?

Anyway, she looked more than well, that's for sure. No rejection: not now her Level 3 status has been ascertained and the stress chamber awaits her. Tomorrow, maybe the day after. I'm not in any hurry. Now, let's think about what to do with the rest of the day.

Abortions

November 20, 1964
Semipalatinsk Military Base Balapan
Bunker 117 – Common Room 47

It's hard to describe what happened yesterday. I can't find the right words. *A slaughterhouse.* The bureaucrats are breathing down our necks. They've shut us all in this huge room, while we wait to be interrogated. I'm writing this in the bathroom, and there's a Red Army brute just outside, guarding the door—never seen him before here in the Bunker. They had a squadron rush in from Moscow. They call them the "cleaners," and they're notorious. *Things have gotten ugly.*

In a few seconds, that guy is going to knock on the door with the stock of his assault rifle, hurrying me up. I'll have to slip the journal back in my pants, and go out and join the others. I need time to collect my thoughts.

November 21, 1964
Semipalatinsk Military Base Balapan
Bunker 117

My stomach is still upside-down. Two days ago, the abortions managed to escape from their cages on Floor -7, slaughtering two guards, taking their weapons, and wreaking havoc in the East Wing.

Luckily, they couldn't get here—to the labs and the experimentation area—so, for once, the Bunker's meticulous security protocols have been good for something. We survived thanks to the compartmentalized tunnel system connecting all of Balapan's areas. The security hatches clenched their teeth, isolating the monster-infested corridors.

But what we saw, through the CCTV, we cannot forget. *There are so many.*

We don't work together here. We don't pool information. We're isolated from the other scientists, each of us working with limited team members—always including the hired telltale of the day. Chatty parrots, big and conspicuous; or magpies dressed in white coats as novice researchers, who don't just sink their hypocritical beaks in shiny things, but hoard photographs of papers, personal notes, and then they flutter back to Command, eager for their reward. That's the murderous wildlife of Balapan for you. You risk being pumped up with water every day, down in the grim chamber of comrade Rostok, who marks a notch on his left leg prosthesis for each heretic scientist he treats. He could never use his glass eye for that—a gift from a mission in south-east Asia—there wouldn't be room enough.

Who knows if that story is true; they talk about him as if he is the devil himself…bad and ugly. But that's probably just another internal-propaganda ruse.

Might be—a rumor to keep us afraid, like the boogieman of our childhood—and yet many colleagues disappeared for real. We counted ourselves when we went to Moscow on leave, little more than a month ago. On our return we were five fewer than those who boarded the bus at the beginning of this adventure. Before segregation.

Little information is transmitted, especially about other teams' progress; our ears hear only what little is needed to create an atmosphere of competition. But that's the Soviet Way to approach the Cold War, so no surprise there. And now, considering what happened, it doesn't really matter.

The abortions, abnormal specimens who didn't succeed with K liquid plutonium, showed unsuspected drives and behaviors. It wasn't only that they tried to escape their cages, assaulting guards and technicians; what was inexplicable (and gruesome) was the anthropophagic instinct they exhibited, lacking any scientific explanation.

It really doesn't make sense, considering those wretches' treatment protocol. Rejection—the "genetic plague"—was foreseeable and observed in 7% of the subjects. But rejection should simply be the antechamber of netherworld for all abortions. After all, they weren't dubbed that for no reason. But apparently, there are things much worse than death.

The massacre scenes, live on our screen from the East Wing corridors, revealed—as we already suspected—that the scientific teams haven't been following the same treatment protocol. In fact, there have been no standards, or indeed, many different procedures resulting in extremely varied results. An aggressive approach to reach goals faster—with the complicity of some ruthless colleagues.

Until two days ago, I only had hard data on Konstantin and Boni. In the boy especially, I recorded clear biological and behavioral changes of an adaptation process only partially anticipated. I was surprised by the formation of those cartilage gills on the subject's neck, while the bluish pigmentation was fully expected, and developed by Boni as well.

But the stress chamber—the riskiest step of the whole cycle of genetic manipulation—unleashed further transformative processes in my candidate's genomic gamma. It wasn't his loss of sight that worried me: research had suggested such a scenario, and the first visor prototypes were almost ready for grafting. What I found surprising were the strength and endurance tests, and especially the data relative to his organ and tissue regeneration.

K plutonium was interacting with his systems in profound ways, and Konstantin was becoming something more than a creature able to adjust quickly to high radiation post-nuclear life. Our analyses showed a new-generation human being with hyper-survival resources.

These new features might have been responsible for the odd stretching of the subject's skull, and its consequent interference with his hypothalamus. Of course, I'm not talking about immortality—let's not be absurd—but it would seem our path is leading us that way.

On the face of it, I'm working on the production of super-soldiers for the Red Army, a dirty and patriotic job with too many hard-to-accept compromises—a new one popping up to swallow and digest daily. But deep down, my goal is far greater, farsighted even.

I blame my imagination for conjuring a new atomic Eden against a backdrop of total nuclear conflict, and a couple of perfect humans from whom a different world might be born. My creative rhabdomancy must have grown inside me like a several-kilo cyst. It's gotten worse.

The older I get, the more I feel like a haruspex in white coat, standing among alembics and Bordeaux bottles full of back-up liquid plutonium, looking at the sky, the glassy horizon, waiting for signs of change. For the Green Apocalypse, that radioactive event, the last one.

Von Braun used to wrap up V1 and V2 for his Führer, the former amateur painter so fond of red, while thinking about how to someday reach the moon. He would dream about that silver oval face every night. Instead, my moon is here, on Earth-2, tomorrow's planet, picked clean of oldgen humanity…

Yes. That was all true until two days ago, before we were forced to witness the slaughter in the East Wing. And yet, Konstantin had never shown the slightest anthropophagic drive, despite being much further along in his treatment than those abnormals who mauled the flesh of soldiers and workers. Nor does Boni's demeanor suggest a monster smoldering beneath that smooth, azure beauty.

Will I be devoured, too? By my own chosen ones? Am I forging assassins, serial cannibals? Will they be the ones ruling the brave new world, only to die off when they eat one another, leaving final dominion to the rats?

I don't think that's a likely scenario: the creatures I saw, those feeding on human flesh, have very little in common with my brave specimens. Sure, the CCTV showed abortions with gills similar to Konstantin's, but they also showed other extraneous anatomic features.

The skulls of some of the subjects looked translucent, as though their bone had given way to much lighter structures. But the low quality of those images couldn't be trusted. An autopsy could shed some light on the matter, though I doubt anybody here loathes their life so much as to open a hatch to try and recover the casualties. The horde waits for a new moving target, and for an opportunity to spread everywhere.

Anyway, the "cleaners" will be in control by now, and they wouldn't allow any funny business, not after managing to seal the North Wing—thanks to the sacrifice of many men—in order to secure other areas of the Bunker.

Some of the escaped abnormals had bulges on their abdomens and backs. They must contain fluid, probably an attempt by the human body to isolate surplus K plutonium.

That's all we can really say, with only a few minutes of images available—and considering the extreme brutality of the scene, which was hardly consistent with scientific observation. The guardians of our monastery, the bureaucrats shut in their control-room, turned their monitors off, leaving us to throw up in peace.

None of us—besides the guards, may they rest in peace— knew anything about the real conditions suffered by those isolated subjects. It was brought about by an inconsistent treatment protocol. No standards: we're a factory of monsters and angels.

We have everything down here.

DECEMBER 2, 1964
SEMIPALATINSK MILITARY BASE
BLOCK 4 MEETING ROOM – CONTAINMENT AREA

Despite the massacre in the East Wing, the brass-headed bureaucrats decided to continue with our experiments as if nothing had happened, even with a whole area of the Bunker still chock-full of the screaming things. Maybe they hope that sooner or later those wretches, forcibly turned into next-gen cannibals, will croak from thirst or starve to death, isolated as they are in those bloodied halls; or that they'll eat each other. Considering the scenes captured on screen, this last hypothesis seems the most likely. But I have no way of knowing what's happening out there.

I can only guess.

What's certain is that Semerov came in this morning with a funeral face and swollen eyes, telltale signs of Moscow's thoughts about the *incident.* Yes, that's what they're calling it. *An incident.*

This time, the General hadn't had time for breakfast. And gone was the disturbing, crooked smile (stuffed with the too-white dentures) that he typically uses to preach optimism and patriotism—and, above all, to wring some bullshit out of the project teams for the Kremlin. Not so different from a chef forced to cover a bland dish with creative garnish. No substance: cherry tomatoes sculpted into small water lilies, and camo-color mousses to put out the olfactory fires of rot. His reassurances are as fake as his teeth. His medals, though, look real enough.

Everything is under control; the East Wing will be soon cleaned up and operational again. So, gentlemen, let's resume our work. Seems to me you've got everything you need. But I understand you're in shock after the incident, so I had some caviar brought in, luxury stuff...a little relaxation of the rules to restore our spirits. We're behind schedule: I expect immediate results. An incident isn't a good excuse to slack off.

That's what he said, more or less… words spat out rapidly, with little conviction this time. Playing it down is part of the procedure, whenever the big shots need to save their asses.

But then, as Semerov snapped his fingers, soldiers in coarse waiter outfits entered two-by-two, trays full of caviar on their shoulders. We shook off our lethargy at the useless meeting and took advantage of it. Self-denial or fasting certainly wasn't going to make things better at that point.

We weren't all there, though, with our jaws and bellies working, swallowing the good stuff after vomiting our souls out before those cursed scenes: only those who were still operational. In Soviet terms: the ones who'd survived the purge.

We counted ourselves again. A few more colleagues were missing, probably eliminated immediately after the incident. Those responsible for the disaster—the animators of those beasts—must have enjoyed a romantic date with Rostok; Rostok *the drowner.* I imagine him carving new notches in his prosthesis, like a Great War flying ace decorating the fuselage of his craft with a skull, or a star, for each enemy airplane shot down.

At least five of us were missing from the headcount; but Professor Kireyev was still there, his snout sunk in the General's caviar, even though his conscience is among the dirtiest. He's the stepfather of Boris—the project's wonder subject—and his little playmate, Anja. My eminent colleague must have someone watching his back, otherwise he would have been first in line to meet Rostok.

I suspect Kireyev follows non-standard protocols. I'm not saying he's some new Doctor Frankenstein, but I'm sure he's behind several of those feral specimens; he must have pushed their organisms beyond the limit, in order to shake off the competition as soon as possible.

I've known him since Lomonosov, where you would rarely spot him: except when he was busy boastfully presenting scientific publications which he supported with cryptic research and minimal experimental data. *Hot air.* He knew how to play dirty with the numbers and stats; he could demonstrate that Earth was flat, or that the Yankees only ate bread and onions and were scourged by third-world plagues. He could persuade the most attentive audience that the rich, blooming, fat and free American citizens were in fact an invention of the Party enemies: nothing more than a well-conceived and expensive ruse, spread through the propaganda of TV. Fake cities, prop buildings, and actors playing up their wealth and democracy.

There's another pretty word. *Democracy.*

Considering recent events I'd better get back to work, unless I wish to drink Rostok's Elixir of Short Life. So be it; I still have time to digest the General's caviar and his salty arrogance. Anyway, I couldn't put off treating of the girl from Kiev too long, not without putting her life at risk, and especially her mutation.

Boni, my white peach, is now shut in her cell like all the other still-uncorrupted specimens, the chosen ones marked Level 3 and 4. I've just gone by the containment area to see her. After the incident, any contact with our candidates was forbidden—they've been left to themselves—but now we've been re-authorized to carry on the brood; and to have the eggs hatch as soon as possible. Semerov's codeword: *Field-tests, field-tests, and field-tests.*

Re-reading this mad-dash journal, I realize, all of a sudden, in the few moments I have no eyes on me—no magpies or KGB-trained camo bears—that I've written precious little about Boni, speaking only about my feelings for her.

After all, she's the protagonist of these pages, directly or indirectly. I must fix that. I don't know how much longer I'll have, how much ink I'll be able to use before being "normalized." The bureaucrats, Rostok and the East Wing monsters, are always lurking, like bombs primed in our underwear. Let's get to it, before it's too late.

Boni was sixteen years old when they brought her to the Bunker; it's been over two years since that night, but I remember it perfectly, as though it were yesterday. Some things are carved on our memory deeper than others. Boni, dirty and bruised that day, was more beautiful than St. Sophia's Cathedral.

She wasn't from the nearby villages or small towns, like Konstantin and all the others; she came from Kiev, where, to eke out a living, she sold herself in a whorehouse for high-ranking officials and Politburo members. Yes, a prostitute, a daughter of the

Dnepr, both hot and ice-cold, like the summers and winters of her city. Her mother, apparently, had entrusted her when she was yet to become "woman" to one of the many Red Army recreational centers. A daughter of the Dnepr has a biological, human matrix, but she's still an illegitimate. *Social classifications*, cutting off your future at the knees.

And so her mother, a quick and pragmatic woman, simply took advantage of her daughter's loveliness to get something. *A B-class flat?*

Who knows? Boni tenses up, about these matters; she doesn't want to talk about it. Who knows how it really went—how much can you really trust the stories of a teenage girl sequestered in a lab? But on the subject of the whorehouse, with its high-profile clientele, she didn't lie. After her arrival, I received a phone call from the Kremlin. Better not to use names, this time… I'm not a coward, and what I'm writing is proof enough to get me killed. But I never want Boni to pay the price for this story, should some busybody ever send these pages on microfiche to the powers that be.

People are quick to vanish, here, should they happen to taint the reputation of someone with silk socks—and she can't evaporate from my life, not now. After her short career between the bedsheets, the whorehouse can do without her (in certain circles, a kid quickly turns from charming muse and Lolita to awkward, depreciated second-hand goods), very easily replacing her with something new; it's not the same for me. As the years go by, I grow ever more attached to things, turning my nose up at the new. Not quite the right disposition, for a scientist, let alone one blessed with my rhabdomancy for the future. But that's different. Boni is different, too, different from everything else, *everyone* else. A solo of survival.

I kept telling my wife this as well, every time I visited, the time I was supposed to spend with my family, putting aside work at least for a couple of days a month. Until I made her loathe Boni. And until Lada began to feel jealous. She was a teenager like Boni, and she feared that the other—so alive, too alive—could take her place in my heart, or that she could take something away from her, anyway. Bitterly, that's exactly how it ended up, and it was my daughter who changed the course of things, that day in the pools, where she talked me into boiling her alive to become my atomic Eve, the first, the chosen one. Before Boni, in her place.

But I'm making my usual mistake, writing too much about my feelings, and too little about my girl from Kiev, who cannot be just a mirror, an empty reflection of my crumbled fatherhood. The only picture I have of her— taken back when she was registered and put on file at the Bunker sorting center—is the bookmark I use for this journal. Perhaps, it will get lost someday, flying away, together with my sins toward other tunnels, where monsters won't be sealed in East or West Wings.

I'm trying to capture, to write down in print, this face before me: fearful, livid, and yet brash…she has always reminded me of Manet's Olympia. Her black bowl cut, her so-white skin, a leather lace tight around her throat with a small aquamarine hanging from it—probably fake.

The mark of her whorehouse, or a customer's gift? Or maybe that stone marks her affiliation to the creatures of the Dnepr, holding a few drops of that water impregnated with many stories, billions in every molecule. Her eyes, black like the ink drawing her, are sudden holes, bent like the backs of almonds on her pale skin; and raised, so proud, by unseen hooks, twin puffs of purple traced by a two-bit eyeliner.

Sometimes, when I look at this picture, Coltrane sits beside me—an elegant ghost of few words—pulling his shiny saxophone from beneath his ribs, and he starts playing *My Favorite Thing*, letting his magic, clandestine music echo through these stone walls, round and round on the vinyl grooves of my memory. But in time, the stylus begins to skip, to forget, and that's when the heretic Ozram resurrects it whole for me, making it run thinly along the phone cable. A sort of inter-curtain tunnel dug from the scratches of sound. Jazz is like oil, spreading all around; it gets to your knees, and then it rises farther. A thick Yankee trap, a flood of glue for thoughts.

That's when Boni doesn't remain helpless—between the four corners of this by-now dead image—she comes to life, though to my eyes only. She comes out of the rectangle of the photo, with all the budding grace of her petite body, stepping over the impossible, the paper edges and the rubber bands of time, and sits on my knees, grabs my hand, steers it on the pages for a few lines. I let her do it, a sign my loneliness. Here's what she's writing now, through my fingers:

You look at me, what do you see? You cannot see. You cannot really touch me. You cannot know. You cannot feel the saliva on your skin, the cigarette embers, the sweat and wet screams slipping over you like another bed sheet, there in the soldiers' beds.

And then she's gone, every time, making me fear that she doesn't really exist outside my rotten head, where there's a black hole to be filled every day.

And then I'd go to the experimentation area, by night, not giving a fuck about the curfew, to see her sleeping in her cot locked in her accommodation, squeezing her eyes against memories still too fresh, or biting her lips and stirring her thighs to flee from something. Ten centimeters of plate glass between her and me, when the blue lights of the corridors summon darkness and take her away out of my hands.

But at least I know she really exists.

JANUARY 11, 1964
SEMIPALATINSK MILITARY BASE
BALAPAN BUNKER 117 – SOUTH WING

The genetic plague has spread, and we're in the middle of a full-fledged epidemic. We lost control of the West Wing, where the experimentation area, our labs, the stress chambers, the pools, and Level 3 subjects' accommodations are.

Almost all of the specimens suffered unexpected mutations. An abnormal biological process, very different from that affecting the "abortions," who are still sealed in the East Wing. Now we're dealing with next-gen creatures, real killing machines with superhuman capabilities.

We can no longer talk about mere rejection: we have created a new species; blind anthropophagic predators, able to regenerate their damaged tissues. They should have been our super-soldiers, our human land fleet for when everybody else would be forced to take shelter underground.

But tables were turned in less than forty-eight hours: we used to be smug demiurges, lighting the atomic spark in chosen subjects; now we're nothing but easy prey. We're not the ones pushing the buttons anymore, and the bureaucrats have already taken flight aboard a flock of helicopters.

This time, we didn't only get to watch gruesome CCTV images, feeling sick in front of a monitor rack; we were in the middle of the upheaval, chased, bitten, mauled. A crazy run to get out of a funnel of death, through pieces of our colleagues scattered everywhere, bullets shooting wildly, and screams of hunt and dread. I still have a bit of somebody's brain on my white lab coat, and my eye is bleeding. But I'm among the lucky ones.

A second slaughter, with only a few survivors from among the scientific staff, technicians and security people. Hundreds of souls are buried forever down here, torn apart in chunks of varying sizes. The assault started suddenly, as though those creatures were linked to one another through an alien radio. Their new mutations had become apparent over a period of about twelve hours. But someone, at some point, blew the telepathic trumpet of war. Hell, if you believe in such a place, can't be worse than what I've seen. Those creatures' attraction for human flesh—brain especially—*must* have a scientific explanation; but under these conditions, it's hard to think. And I don't even know how I managed to put these few lines together.

The soldiers hurried us to the South Wing of this damned facility, their own territory, while waiting for orders. The few subjects not showing signs of the new mutation were brought here, too. They're shut all together in a warehouse, watched closely by the twitchy, brawny men from the "cleaners" squad. Their camo suits have also collected bloody mementos of the attack.

Among the chosen ones locked there, there are Konstantin and Boni, Boris and Anja—Kireyev's couple— and four more candidates in advanced stages, about whom I know nothing. They all look stable, for now; but for the last few hours we haven't been able to check for new data on their K plutonium exposition curve and molecular assimilation. Their fate hangs in the balance.

I couldn't bear to see Boni turn into a sort of cannibalistic, flesh-digging queen bee; her perfect, well-proportioned body made ungainly by those hideous, glowing chest sacs characterizing the new abnormals—much more dangerous and capable than the previous ones.

Blind assassins hungry for human meat, they're just one step away from immortality. The uprising of our blue demons has just started. I'm afraid it's over

JANUARY 12, 1964
HOTEL RADISSON BLU – KIEV

I'm afraid it's over indeed. The surviving scientific staff have been transferred to Kiev, in this hotel monopolized by the bureaucrats and their lackeys. I'm not aware of Boni and Konstantin's fate, nor the other chosen ones who were apparently immune to the genetic plague. At least, until two days ago.

We cannot exit our rooms (all single rooms, but that's not a favor: they don't want us to talk to one another) until we're be summoned to the dining room. So they said.

It seems General Semerov is going to show up in person shortly, to give us an update. I figure the military are having a clean-out, down there in the screaming bunker; I bet they're not messing around this time, hastening to take back the facility and (maybe) allow us to resume our experiments. One massacre after another, that's what Project Prometheus has become.

At a key moment in my candidates' mutation, I was forced to leave them by themselves in that Hell. They may have been moved, too, somewhere safe. Locked and away from prying eyes. After all, they represent a heavy investment for the regime; I don't think they're going to put everybody in the same basket—and then set fire to it with a flamethrower.

But by now anything's possible. Perhaps, Konstantin is currently leading the uprising, shaking his freshly grown sacs...while Boni, with her thin azure cuirass, is biting out the brains of the enemy rearguard.

What am I thinking...truth is, I can't really discard the idea that I've gone completely mad, a slow mental decay that started the very day I landed at the Bunker's mouth. Or maybe everything began to teeter, in my head, that day at the pools, looking at Lada immersed in low-concentration K plutonium that had been watered down in an alchemic cocktail of lipids and accelerants. She had bones as white as snow, and then, when her skin began to show the first cracks, those horrible fissures, unexpected tears glistened among the thick green bubbles of nuclear fried food.

Makes little difference—it's in there I lost my head anyway. Underground.

Afternoon. Semerov still has to show up; the only sign of life here, besides myself—about whom I'm increasingly more suspicious—is the new Rossija 1 channel, with its black-and-white Ministry of Public Education propaganda croaking on the TV screen. Big deal. I'm astounded. I'm keeping that thing turned on to hear any sound other than my short breaths, the shaking hiccup of the elevator, and the snow melting under the tires of passing cars down on the road. Right, snow—but not perfectly white like Lada's bones. Snow and mud and, on the edges, misery hiding inside cardboard boxes, Z-class flats where somebody's thoughts are smoking through the holes of their makeshift lairs.

I wonder what the others are doing.

Evening. Still no General and no info. An hour ago, I heard knocking at my door; I sprang to my feet and rushed to open it. *Was I finally about to learn Konstantin and Boni's fate? Was there a bus ready, to take us to the helicopter pads?*

Nothing of the sort. Just a waitress with a tray full of stuff. Of course: dinner for the Bunker scientists. We don't officially exist, but we must eat nonetheless. We're not traditional ghosts: we can't walk through walls, and we get missed-meal cramps like everybody else.

A dish of beetroot soup (can you really do without borsch in Kiev?), just lukewarm and with little lard on the side, accompanied by a sad glass of red wine. Foul stuff.

I felt like speaking to someone, and when I asked the girl her name—as an excuse not to let her escape as soon as she'd set those meager provisions on the small table—I was stricken. *Lada, sir.*

I swallowed the other words I had in my mind, and I watched her go out and close the door, dropping the curtain on the last slice of her strange smile. Coincidences are always part of statistics, of the dragging and hopping of reality. They are empiric facts, and as a scientist I should be well aware of that.

But, for fuck's sake, this story gets weirder and weirder. I'm not sure if I should pinch my leg to check if I'm really awake or begin to really question my sanity.

Night. I can't sleep. Writing is a blessing. I can no longer do without it. I'd like to get out, flee, let my anxiety run on the streets until its exhausted.

The Art Museum is a stone's throw from here. I'd like to be a fly, or any other tiny winged creature, able to enter the building through some hidden crack, drift among a thousand colors, stains and turned-off galleries, and finally alight on the cheek of Borovikovsky's portrait of Maria Lopukhina. That woman…she's the nearest thing to this picture of Boni I always carry with me, in here, as a charm between these pages.

That face, her pallor, the impudent gaze. Just her, on canvas. I saw that painting twenty years ago, during my first visit to Kiev for a conference. I didn't know I'd met my eternal return in flesh and bone.

JANUARY 13, 1964
HOTEL RADISSON BLU, KIEV

Still here, in this room. But it won't be for much longer.

This morning, the General summoned us all into the dining room, set as though for a wedding reception. He talked for a few minutes; he looked confused as he eyed his scarce audience (each time we see each other, we count ourselves; and each time we are fewer), as though he feared some bureaucrat might be camouflaged among us, somebody ready to phone Siberia to book him a room in a reconditioning center—accommodations for big shots like him, with iron bars on the windows and saunas equipped with electroshock facilities.

But our attention whipped away from the small improvised dais—squeezing good old Semerov's abundant sides—to the table on his left, some distance from the others: there sat a pair of rusty officials, a hungry driver, a still medal-less orderly, and our friend Rostok. *Him, here in Kiev.* The drowner looks like another person, dressed in a suit and tie like that. You could almost be tempted to shake his hand and exchange some bad-taste jokes between one vodka and the next. Only his glass eye betrayed him, somehow. There were no armed military visible, which was pretty disturbing. When you can't even see them, it's always a bad sign.

The General—who kept wiping his forehead with his handkerchief—straightened his back and got right to the point. He told us that the situation at the Bunker would be fixed in a few days; that our stay at the Radisson Blu would be over soon; even going so far as to say that we *should enjoy this nice vacation*; and finally, that we'll be back to work within the week, along with our teams. What's left of them, of course.

Then, catching his breath, he spat out more fragments of truth. Project Prometheus, apparently, would be transferred to a new location, for security reasons. *So, Boni, Konstantin, and the others... Are they still alive?*

Then the double doors on the left side of the room were shut, one after another like dominoes, by sketchy types who popped out of thin air, dressed up waiters with too tight uniforms but hired-gun faces.

Was it time for some important revelation? Or were they about to do us all in? It's always a thin line, in these cases. I stared at Rostok, who kept gulping wine from the bottle, while eyeing us one by one. *Was he counting us, too?*

After a short pause, the General revealed the mystery. We would resume our duties at the under-construction nuclear plant Vladimir Il'ič Lenin in Chernobyl—one of the greatest and most futuristic Soviet projects, meant to host the first reactor a few years from now. People talk about it as the breakthrough which will tip the Cold War balance.

In short, we're headed to the Soviet answer to the Yankee "Nevada Test Site—51," ever more bustling with activity and secret tactical projects.

Project Prometheus must be considered outdated; we're all now on board Unit Zero at the plant, another thing that shouldn't exist...at least, not yet. We're going to have new labs and all kinds of cutting-edge equipment.

We've been experimenting, in the Bunker; now, it's time to get down to business. The regime wants *operativity*. He used that word twice, our General, pointing his index finger upward, maybe hoping we'd understand that his speaking mouth, his thoughts, and all the invisible lines hooked to his face muscles—fishing his very soul—were pulled by our great leader and his tight circle of bureaucrats with their Mercedes Benzes and personal dachas with indoor swimming pools.

Unit Zero...

JANUARY 15, 1964
HOTEL RADISSON BLU, KIEV

Night. I'll be moved tomorrow to the Chernobyl plant.

So Liev (I only know his first name) told me a few hours ago, introducing himself as the General's spokesman as he poked his sharp nose into this room. That bony guy didn't look at my face, just kept talking sotto voce his eyes scanning all around. What did he think he'd find in here?

He reassured me about Konstantin and Boni. What a relief. *No rejection, you'll be able to continue your work.* He didn't waste any more breath. But when I asked him about my team—Helena and Oleg, whom I haven't seen here though they survived the second massacre—he turned and threw me a vulture gaze; a sated vulture, but a dangerous one nonetheless. *No rejections, you'll be able to continue your work*, he repeated. I raised my hands, what else could I do?

Once he was gone—he didn't need any words to recommend that I maintain the utmost secrecy—and the disgusting trail of his cheap aftershave had vanished completely, I go to the door and lean my ear against it, like a redskin setting up an assault, waits for the vibration of an incoming train on the railway, far away.

The door of this room has never been locked, though we were "kindly" asked not to wander around the hotel. Certain suggestions—especially those uttered in a smile by somebody's "spokesman"—must always be listened to. And then again, I figured there were guards everywhere, either placed in the open with the usual Soviet smugness or hiding in the shadows.

And the Radisson Blu has seemed like it was haunted since its seizure. At least from what little I saw, walking through the half-empty stomach of this structure going to the great dining room.

I'd always done as instructed; but a few minutes ago, I opened the door and craned my neck out in the hall. Nothing. Silence. After all, it was three in the morning— what was I supposed to find, or see? I moved a few steps toward the elevators, but I was scared away by somebody moaning, and I squeezed myself against the wall.

At the far end of the hall, I saw that bastard Rostok, followed by another, huge-headed man—never seen him before—pushing someone into a room... He had Rostok's hand on his mouth. *Goodbye to my unknown colleague...*

I hopped back into my own room. I closed the door and resumed breathing. All clear: they're cleaning up, exterminating monsters in the Bunker, and excess scientists in this damned hotel.

Holes, Heads, and Caviar

January 16, 1965
Vladimir Il'ič Lenin nuclear plant, Černobyl'
Unit Zero – Accommodations 3B

The plant doesn't exist yet.

On our way in, close to the village of Kopaci, all we could see was an immense area cleared of forest and swept by the icy wind. No sign of foundations, digs, surveying. *So…where was this infamous Unit Zero? And the labs, the cutting-edge facilities and all the bonanza promised by the General?*

At first, I suspected I was in for an ugly end: it really looked like one of those places in the middle of nowhere, where you execute somebody away from prying eyes. But things didn't add up… *All this act, the performance of the hotel and the trip from Kiev escorted like heads of state, just to do in three poor scientists?*

Correct, there are only three of us left; no need to count anymore.

Rostok must have dealt with our other colleagues who'd been scuttling about the Radisson Blu. I can't forget that night in the hotel hall, when that bastard and his huge headed mate disposed of one of us.

Of course, there was the official version. No question needed, the answer was already prepared: *The others have already been transferred to another location. No change in your schedule: as soon as you get to your destination, you'll find new assistants and a brand-new staff.* So Captain Demidov—chief of our escort—had announced, while urging us aboard two bulky ZiL-111 (mocking Cadillacs) idling in front of the hotel. Like heads of state, as I said, even if dawn was just appearing and it was as 60 Holes, Heads, and Caviar cold as all Hell. Cosy departure time.

So, all I could do was take my place on the back seat of the first vehicle with old Professor Urgant, while Kireyev climbed aboard the other car. We were the last "captains" of the Bunker, the shapers of the new Prometheus, survivors of monsters and bureaucrats' purges. Only three brains still switched on, though clouded by now, out of a staff initially comprising over ninety souls, among them assistants, researchers, and project leaders.

At the plant, after a few minutes' bewilderment—it was better before when we couldn't see—I understood that my scientific career was destined to continue underground. They weren't going to get rid of us, and that was something, considering the surreal atmosphere.

They drove us to an almost-invisible access: a low steel dome, more or less at the center of that huge area scraped clean of every life sign, frozen like all the rest...including my feet, and I believe my colleagues', too, unprotected by military combat boots but clad in common walk shoes.

Well, it wasn't as though we had much with us at the Radisson Blu, and those guys didn't certainly bother to gear us up for the occasion.

That thing there in the middle, well-camouflaged by ice-white brush strokes, was a gigantic hydraulic hatch, like a submarine's. Then, two ladders led down a well, until you set your feet on the floor of the first underground level. Branches lead off toward different areas from a central node with square elevators that could fit twenty people, apparently meant to carry equipment and personnel to the many levels and crannies of that hive.

From one bunker to another...luckily, I've never been claustrophobic.

They escorted us to the accommodations for the scientific personnel without too many explanations; they would show us the labs later, and everything else we needed to resume our work.

Is Boni down here, with Konstantin and the others?

They must be, of course, but I'm restless; I want to see them right away, and check on their mutation state. And instead, here I am in my room, imagining more than knowing. At least, I've been allowed to make my usual two phone calls.

This time, though cramped, my room is well-equipped: it even comes with a personal phone that can be activated through the facility switchboard. Knowing the characters in charge of security, this is no comfort...they just don't want us wandering about the facility too much.

From what little I've managed to see, there's so much more going on around here, than just our project.

Unit Zero, nice name; it sounds like something already in an advanced experimentation phase, though officially one of those non-existent things, like the plant itself. But something that everyone is eventually going to see; at the right time, it will be released into the public domain. Down here...it's another story. *An underground reactor? Or some other contraption?*

I'm making my phone calls, now.

I already knew I'd be wasting my first call—that was a given. This time, Klara didn't call me a worm, but it wasn't necessarily a good thing; she didn't even sound like she could be bothered insulting me. I've been demoted from worm to nothing. I'm dead to her now, that much is clear.

Luckily, I could always count on old Ozram... I missed his nonsense, and I wanted to enjoy the last additions to his selection of inter-curtain music, those songs I try hard to keep in my head, which feels too empty sometimes. Loneliness seems silent, but that's a trap. If you really listen, you can hear its notes—and it's so easy to become its prey.

This time, Ozram—

I was interrupted. An unexpected visitor. I barely had time to hide the journal under my pillow. Kireyev—nobody else—the bureaucrats' pet, the last person I was expecting 62 Holes, Heads, and Caviar to see here in my new lair.

He'd never so much as looked at me before. A matter of political, more than scientific, hierarchy. And I've never been in the good graces of people sitting in control rooms or drawing new maps on the pool tables of their personal dachas.

That dandy leaped into my room without even knocking, his eyes wide. *Pavel, my old friend, what are you up to?*

Had he seen the journal? No, he seemed interested in something else. It wasn't long before he spilled the beans, cutting courtesies to a minimum.

I've always respected your work, you know that. But of course, I remember all too well. He would always keep me at a distance at Lomonosov, dodging me like an annoying bug, preferring to be surrounded by crowds of adoring students, beautiful women, and party officials— those fashionably dressed, mustachioed recruiters combing the university all day long, to haul nets full of wriggling young brains to be trained, or lobotomized. Kireyev was the first, to his credit, to treat me like a worm.

Sorry, Klara, see? You weren't that original, after all.

Then, the genius began beating around the bush, as you might in a courteous meeting between old schoolmates, often repeating the term collaboration—a real burst-fire, his voice pitching higher to reinforce the emphasis on that pretty word—in the middle of his generic spiel.

Collaborate. He was preparing the ground. For what? I understood it all, reality engulfing me at once, when he dropped his mask and invited a man to join us. He was bundled up in a heavy jacket; his huge, disproportioned head covered by a hood. Apparently, my second guest had been waiting for the right signal outside in the corridor outside my door. But right after that, a third guest materialized…a "piece" of guest, to be more precise.

And then…things got really tough.

I'm upset; both for the revelations which suddenly shed light on many things—how things ended up in the Bunker, overcrowded with first- and second-gen abnormals—and (especially) for the brutality shown by Kireyev, a scientist, and his butcher friend to solve a "little problem." That's how they defined it.

I can't keep writing, not now; soon, they'll bring me my dinner (conviviality seems to be ruled out, here as well) and it's best they find me with a slightly more composed face than the one I'm wearing now. I've looked at myself in the mirror. I'm yellow with disgust. And there's Boni, too...involved in this ever-darkening story. I'm afraid and grossed out. Many, too many things right at this moment.

Tomorrow, assuming I don't end badly tonight— not counting the already-scheduled nightmares—I'll try and write down the enormities I've just heard (and witnessed). I still can't deal with it. Who knows, maybe morning will come upon me, cool, whispering in my ear that I've simply gone mad. A clear, well-defined acknowledgment, before I leap between the legs of delirium.

After all, it would be the less painful solution.

JANUARY 17, 1965
VLADIMIR IL'IČ LENIN NUCLEAR PLANT, ČERNOBYL'
UNIT ZERO – ACCOMMODATIONS 3B

It's all clear, now, and I can see things straight. After a breather...

Two days ago, they blew up the Balapan Bunker— creatures, tunnels and all. Problem solved. Or better: totally disintegrated, courtesy of one hundred and thirty kilotons of explosives. Right, no half-hearted efforts around here.

Officially, it was the Chagan Test, pride and joy of the undersurface Peaceful Nuclear Explosions program (PNEs). In short, in place of the underground facility formerly hosting Project Prometheus, there's now a nice four-hundred-meter crater. As Kireyev told me about this incredible "giant purge," hot from the plutonium grill, he spread his arms pincers-like, sneering. *Are you surprised? What planet do you live on? Didn't you know about the PNEs?*

The bastard was acting smart, and he wasn't funny in the least...but better to keep listening to him without question. He had no reason for telling me tall tales. With all his political hooks, and his fame as a regular at the bureaucrats' (spicy) salons, he always knows better than me—about everything. Not as a scientist, but as regime player, heir apparent to a caste with shiny shoes and bloodied soles. It's people like him who climb high, up to the flared lofts of the Kremlin.

It will become a nice lake, Pavel, the first atomic lake, he continued, having a ball wrong-footing me, messing with my head. But that wasn't bullshit either, not even an exaggeration. The explosion site (the ceiling of my first underground assignment) was the dry bed of the Chagan River; the creation of an artificial lake and a network of irrigation canals seems to make sense. As they say, *two birds with one stone.*

Of course, that's brilliant, I answered, waiting for new revelations that would leave me agape. My eminent colleague seemed in a chatty mood. I was about to know why.

Good, a new hole at Semipalatinsk, and the usual collateral nobody gives a damn about. So what's new? Why did that man—staring at me with wide eyes— look as if he was still waiting to drop his ace in the hole? What else was there?

Show it to him, Boris. Pull it out. With these words, which he addressed to his mysterious hooded companion, he began his performance turning my room into a small circus of horrors; he couldn't wait any longer, he wanted to throw his pretty red ace—hearts—in my face and end the game.

Boris, the apple of his eye (now the odd proportions of that head are clear), nodded, shoving his hands in his backpack and pulling out a cut-off human head, wrapped in a transparent plastic bag; *Professor Urgant*...that piece of man was him, his plume of white hair mottled with frost (they must had kept him cool); a chilly, immaculate scream, frozen before it was uttered, and his round spectacles with their turtle frames lacking a lens. *Such horror, but why...*

I thought my turn had come, and I felt an imaginary snare tightening around my neck. *What would they use to cut me?* But Kireyev was unperturbed; he barely held back the sardonic smile pulling at the corners of his mouth. Sitting on the bed, he lit a cigarette, and gestured Boris to bugger off with his grim parcel—the big guy kept twisting it in his hands, weighing the brain of the old professor. *So, I wasn't about to end up like that, too. Not immediately, at least.*

Together with a puff of smoke, my sadistic colleague came out with all the rest. Quickly, like a viper baring its fangs and driving its poison deep, bringing its enemy close to death. Just a step away, on the doorstep. A painful warning.

He didn't want to collaborate, the old fool. That word again (collaborate), so cherished by Kireyev. *Luckily, you're cast in a very different mold*, he added then, watching my reactions. I managed to keep myself controlled, despite it all; what else could I do but listen, comprehend, think how to keep my head attached to my neck, how to face the situation.

I was about to discover that my maneuvering space was more limited than I'd hoped; and it involved Boni and Konstantin.

The Kremlin pet had it all planned; he just needed me, in my role as dynamo—far from second fiddle— and everything would work out.

The bastard's cobweb was revealing itself in full, carefully weaved, down to the smallest detail. That shiny-shoed man has a great talent for adaptation... one of the basic requirements of our super-soldier candidates.

He confirmed that the so-called Unit Zero of the plant—the black stomach digesting us both—hosts the surviving subjects; but I had no doubt about that, it couldn't be otherwise, or I wouldn't be aboard this second phase of the project. *Operativity!* the General had roared at the Radisson Blu.

What I had no inkling of was that Konstantin and Boni were the only ones to last—undamaged and without rejection—through the genetic plague which had turned the Balapan Bunker into a slaughterhouse. Until the final boom.

What had happened to the other surviving subjects? The ones moved here? *Was it all bullshit, what they'd told us at the hotel during that wedding lunch?*

And what was Boris doing around the plant, outside the hyper-guarded area where the last specimens of our atomic flock were kept? More than a super-soldier, one of the chosen ones, by now he looked like a hit man doing my colleagues' dirty work. An evolved cutthroat, a next-gen Rostok.

What they told me before we left for the plant (as I keep calling this place, although it's just a big hole in the belly of the Earth) wasn't all bullshit. According to my bloodthirsty colleague, six subjects—three couples— were initially transferred here. Beside Konstantin and Boni, Boris and Anja were in, and the two specimens entrusted to old Urgant, too: Ermil and Bella. They had all achieved at least Level 3 in the treatment, but only Konstantin and Boris had undergone the stress chamber, the link toward field-testing and becoming ready-to-deploy in a highly-radioactive combat zone... like that lingering, thick choking cloud on the stained sky over Semipalatinsk, soon to drift—pushed by the propellers of air currents—for thousands of kilometers, contaminating, transforming, killing with the silencer of cancer.

So, what happened then?

Apparently—but I'm relying on that weasel's words—after the specimens were moved here to the Hole, they were temporarily entrusted to a small staff of young scientists. But the genetic plague continued to work inside their bodies, mutating them, while nobody suspected anything, as they waited for the second phase of the project to begin, with us—the captains—again at the helm of those by-now half-alien DNA helices. We were the only ones knowing every detail: they were our brood, after all. And the traditional, human part of those creatures was by now negligible. It was in the service of evolution.

Of course, those incompetents didn't know how to read the data, which differed from anything they'd ever seen in their short research careers, and they couldn't even manage a simple transfer. During the few days they'd had to look after those so-precious specimens and check their organic processes in real time, they were deceived by genetic aberrations that took root, malignant, without being noticed.

In fact, there was no trace of those hideous, illfamed glowing sacs—characterizing the second band of abnormals, back in the Bunker tunnels. Those symptoms were by now well-known to everybody. To look for others, for new ones, you'd need an entirely different kind of expertise. And all the while, the bureaucrats were keeping us confined at the Radisson Blu. *Well done!*

Kireyev's wordy account clashed with the spectacle of old Urgant's chopped head, as he enthused over the rest of his story…

Should I believe him? All I could do was humor him while he talked…although, the Kremlin's pet was proving he knew more than me—no surprise there—about both Project Prometheus and this much darker second phase, soon to take place in the buried plant that doesn't exist. Disproportionate foundations, so deep as to tickle the navel of Hell—or whatever there may be down here, at the bottom.

Kireyev had himself observed invisible, internal mutations in Boris, back when we were all gathered at the Radisson Blu (or at least so I thought); these changes marked the destiny of that chosen one, now called "Karakurt" by my colleague. New purpose, from atomic super-soldier to super-killer; new codename for the subject.

The last projections and tests gave him a life expectancy of six months; so much for tissue regeneration.

He'd been put in the stress chamber too soon (I foretold that); and the molecularly grafted K liquid plutonium, after massive radioactive overexposure, had produced an endocrine gland malformation. Microscopic crystals formed, damaging his organism in the new genetic re-engineering.

Boris could no longer become Prometheus, so he'd been given a new task: to serve his Country, for what time he had left, as a killer. He became Karakurt, the character I saw back at the hotel—and together with Rostok, such a nice couple—cut off the heads of colleagues (like old Urgant). And who knows what else?

What else? Kireyev must have read my thoughts, because he immediately lifted the curtain on yet another brutal, horrible edition of this story.

Anja—a Level 3 like Boni—was subject to a horrible, gruesome fate.

The subjects had been transferred to the security rooms of the plant, and each couple isolated from the others. But that had been a mistake. Boris' gland mutations were causing secondary—but far from unimportant—effects, considering the subjects' reclusion. Not only did they decrease his tissue regeneration capability, undermining his adaptability to a radioactive environment (Kireyev assessed a 30% reduction in a few days); but also overloading his amygdala and, obviously, deeply influencing his limbic and sympathetic nervous systems.

Emotions and inner drives were in synaptic short-circuit…and Anja paid the price as she shared her accommodation in the plant "Safe" Zone—another pretty word—with that monster in steady behavioral degeneration. *Karakurt was being born.*

Back in the Balapan Bunker, there'd been talk about a second phase, after the field-tests and the first operational subjects; examining the possibility of reproduction between treated specimens, and also with non-treated human specimens. Boris, drunk with the psychedelic, wild curve of his new sensations, sped things up with Anja who, at Level 3, wasn't fit for mating, at least based on our preliminary studies. A Level 3 specimen is still inchoate, in a transient status, neither human nor atomic (or "promethean," as some colleagues liked to say).

But none of this would faze our new Karakurt.

That moron raped her. He killed her in less than three minutes, Kireyev told me with regret—incredible but true, the sadistic bastard has feelings! Apparently, he'd cared for his atomic Amazon, just like me with my Boni. *Boris' seminal vesicles contained those damn crystals…you can imagine how it ended up…*

It was clear, no need for words. A horrible end for the girl.

And Urgant's couple? The professor's fate had been made all too clear to me, but what about Ermil and Bella? Kireyev no longer seemed in the mood to talk. His loquaciousness had suddenly waned. This time, I had to ask, insist, to complete my understanding of the mosaic of events. A few tiles kept hiding...I needed another to fully grasp the truth of what I was part of, like a stupid cog. Sure, that's the Soviet Way of propagating reality, setting up parallel incomplete versions, with all the smoke and mirrors artfully placed, and booby traps scattered everywhere. Maybe, not even my eminent colleague, after all, knew the whole story.

But he did know about Urgant's couple, and finally I convinced him to tell me. He had another ace in store, black this time, spades or clubs. But it was for later. *Urgant's treatment protocol was different... The old windbag was good. If only he hadn't been such a fool...*

And then more words, confused sentences...a hesitant, sloppy explanation, full of holes; and then, luckily, some facts: Ermil (I remember him... when they brought him to the Bunker, a hulk like the classic circus strongman)—

The red light on the phone flashed—an internal line. I had to answer. I was to join Kireyev in the Safe Zone. I'll see Boni and Konstantin again, at last. I'll work out how to deal with this...

No more time to write, I'll wait for the right moment

JANUARY 18, 1965
VLADIMIR IL'IČ LENIN NUCLEAR PLANT, ČERNOBYL'
UNIT ZERO – ACCOMMODATIONS 3B

I've just come back from the Safe Zone, where I spent thirteen straight hours. And so, my collaboration with that butcher began (could I refuse?). Pretty word, *collaboration.* If only it didn't hide the tail of blackmail in its pants—and of the worst kind. I'm not talking about the safety of my own head (I don't deem it particularly essential at this point), or about its natural position on my neck. I don't feel like writing about it, not yet, because some things burn hard inside. This is enough, for now.

I finally saw Boni and Konstantin again… The first analyses show them in good health. He's almost blind now, and he'll need a visor as soon as possible. But this was expected, and the device is ready to be grafted.

Boni is instead stable at Level 3, and she keeps painting the walls of her secure room in her spare time, when she isn't being cycled through our unending tests and micro-trials. She uses a special paint, this time I caught her doing it: she uses her fingers as brushes, bringing them to her mouth to dip them in her thick green saliva…and then, sometimes, she lowers a hand between her legs, pulling out an ephemeral watercolor orange to extend her limited palette.

But she stopped immediately when she noticed me, jumping to her feet and hiding her arms behind her back, covering her last creation. But there were many others, all around her. Some unexpected, and stunning.

That watered-down, organic orange must come from the blooms growing around her pubis, which I'd already observed a month ago. Clusters of microscopic buds, containing what appeared to be inactive fluids with no function. No comparison with the glowing sacs of the second-series abnormals; sooner or later, we'll discover what they do.

That's where she finds her colors; her own corporeal inks, nothing more. I'd often wondered about that, during my last days at the Bunker, noticing her conjuring those long-necked anthropomorphic figures, with thin bones and empty sockets (the soul-less eyes of Modigliani's works look at you the same way, with disturbing emotional inertia) all over the four steel canvases keeping her locked in. Rough shapes, anatomically disproportioned, linked to one another by tentacles, or flesh coils—but growing finer now, technically and artistically speaking. Could Level 3, through the engines of standard protocol, interfere with new talents?

So much yet to understand and discover.

The labs and equipment of the Safe Zone are as good as promised, and my new team includes—oddly—even a few sharp brains, beside the usual creativity-impaired incompetents, and researcher-posing parrots (flesh and-bone radio spies of the bureaucrats) who hardly understood a single thing I told them during our first briefing.

Should I be satisfied?

Not really. I've resumed working with my subjects, trying to grab the elusive cat of insights by its tail in order to tame it and write a new future. My innate rhabdomancy—an encephalic sonar able to pinpoint, pick up with tweezers, and scan what hasn't a name yet—will be quenched.

But now I must work in tight collaboration with Kireyev. He lost his brood (Anja dead and Boris, expiring Prometheus and rapist, isolated and waiting to be recycled...though his stepfather clearly has the keys for his cage); but my eminent colleague sweet-talked his bureaucrat friends, threatened me (and what concerned me the most: Boni), in order to remain a protagonist in the project. He considered that his right, no matter what.

His plan is simple, straight-forward: to take advantage of my understanding (something eludes him in the mutation process) and then get rid of me, maybe in the same way as poor Urgant.

After all, I'm the only one among the enjoined scientist, who has produced some positive results. If I want to keep my head on my neck, my white coat clean, and avoid Boni being boiled alive in the stress chamber— *Wouldn't it be a shame, Pavel? She's so beautiful*—I must continue to prove myself useful, or better, essential to the Kremlin's pet.

And so now I have to share my intuitions, data, tests and partial results, and trials for new complementary protocols with that bastard. In short, I'll have him breathing down my neck (I think about Urgant's head every time I write this word) throughout the process meant to lead Konstantin and Boni toward illumination—atomic illumination, of course. Level 5, operativity.

I feel sick.

Evening. Another work session with Kireyev, who keeps drooling over Boni. *Is he doing that to keep me vigilant? Or just to rub it in?* I must keep an eye on that sadistic bastard, who recognizes my weak point perfectly.

I've just realized that I still have to write about the ugly end of the candidates raised by poor beheaded Urgant. This time, no Karakurt emerged—Boris' black-seasoned version. The Kremlin's pet took care of them himself. First, he got rid of the old professor—not even allowing him the time to unpack in his quarters here at the plant (*They believe he fled abroad, Kireyev boasted, you just need to put breadcrumbs at the right places for those tin-headed KGB hounds*).

Then, Kireyev tried to force his hand on Ermil and Bella, two still-unstable Level 3s: he shut them in the new stress chambers, just built in this facility. More compact and powerful, geometrically reducing exposition times, apparently. He wanted to overtake me, it's that simple, and quickly. When a star is too bright—and the bureaucrats always watch constellations—you must turn it off; or blind it with something even better.

The bastard used Ermil and Bella as lab rats, not giving a damn about treatment protocol (not the first time he's taken such liberties); he completely skipped the required preparation steps before sending them to the radioactive oven. *Maybe it gave him a 3-4% chance of conjuring up a Level 4, and tying the game with me and my Konstantin?*

That small percentage was more than enough for him. Ermil, probably already sitting on some secondary rejection, exploded inside the chamber after only twelve minutes. They had to use hydrants to clean up the walls and ceilings of the small, airtight structure—Kireyev calls it "the magic box."

Apparently, Bella, survived; but an hour after coming out of the plutonium iron maiden, a gill formed at her breastbone (not on the side of her neck like Konstantin's), and it caused the girl's lungs to quickly collapse. The Kremlin's pet hurried his explanations; he blamed the new stress chambers for his failure. *We'll have to configure them better, dear Pavel... The technicians here aren't certainly the best.*

"Dear Pavel," yes, I'd moved ahead in the bastard's head, promoted from buzzing bug or worm, I've reached the summit: becoming (almost) his equal. But that's just on the surface, he simply needs me, for now. I'm sure that, at the right moment, he'll have my head broken by Karakurt, and he'll shove my brain into a vodka-filled crystal; he'll keep it in his new display of trophies and decorations, full of dust, somewhere near the back.

The man who forged Prometheus, male and female.

Night. The clock says 4:15; I've just emerged from a strange dream. No nightmares tonight, at least for now. The crater of the Chagan Test explosion had been filled with water, and I floated on that transparent, crystal-clear Atomic Lake.

On the shore, in the distance, I glimpsed the outline of a fisherman, his line in the water, waiting for his impossible cobalt dinner. That man is wasting his time, I thought, while taking a few strokes to approach him. But then something bit. The fisherman began pulling and reeling in his catch. Who knows what he used as bait? *Would he pull out a combat boot or a diesel jerry can? Or maybe professor Urgant's chopped head?* There could be nothing alive in there, not even algae (thinking as a scientist in my dreams, too). A question of roentgen.

I got closer, and the figure became clearer until I could make it out quite well. It was me, maybe ten years younger, though at least five meters tall. I called to that gigantic self on the shore, hurrying to join him. But he'd caught his prey, and was freeing the hook from her mouth. *A blue-skinned siren?* Boni, on the shore, could hardly breathe, while the giant shadow of myself sat on a large flat stone and looked at her in silence. Close by now, with the water up to my thighs, I heard her sing.

Karakurt!

February 26, 1965
Vladimir Il'ič Lenin nuclear plant, Černobyl'
Unit Zero

I have neglected the journal this last month.

There are many things to write, now; to digest, as always.

Kireyev holds me ever tighter in his coils. The bastard squeezes hard. A boa constrictor with small red stars in the place of lozenges, I don't know how to describe him better; sometimes, he's about to choke me, making me spit out my very soul—*It would be risky, putting Boni in the stress chamber right away… You know we must reconfigure those magic boxes*—but he knows when to loosen his grip, at the right moment, abruptly going back to that fake friendly demeanor, bearing an acrylic grin and a perfect denture.

Pavel, I couldn't do this without you. I've always admired you.

So, he convinced me (euphemism) to help him graft the visor to his Karakurt. His favorite head-cutter had suddenly gone blind, useless, and soon to be obliterated. The bureaucrats had already put the red stamp on the subject sheet; a failure, both as Prometheus and as temporary assassin. A matter of days, before a team of "cleaners" blows into his cell in the Safe Zone to fix things.

For the Kremlin, nothing would be worse than a secret weapon incarnated—one which keeps misfiring—in the wrong hands. An autopsy would be as bad as the American pictures of the missile installations in Cuba.

We had to work by night on the visor, when the security of the plant relies on only half its personnel (and 80 Karakurt! those on duty dilly-dally with vodka and cards). We hid our intentions by signing a document which we knew to be bombproof to KGB brains: amongst the many useless big words and made-up scientific terms, it ultimately highlighted a single thing in twenty-two pages of rubbish. The necessity of analyzing Boris/Karakurt's DNA—*and testing the visor on him, of course*—in order to guarantee progress with Konstantin and Boni, minimizing risks of regression, molecular rejection, or infections (we underlined that word) caused by the grafting of sight prostheses.

To protect the evolution of our post-atomic Adam and Eve: that's the priority here, even before breathing. As the frown on every portrait of Leonid Il'ič Brežnev hanging in this facility (that doesn't exist) seems to remind us: *Look me in the eye, Comrade.*

My candidates are Soviet assets, and they must be safeguarded as closely as the blueprints of a spy satellite, a picklock for space—all that lies beyond the new world waiting for us, still black and so empty and silent.

They authorized us to proceed. Of that, we had no doubt. If something went wrong with the last couple of candidates available, the project would be suspended and General Semerov would have to pin the last medal on his uniform, and read the destination on a train ticket delivered by an official in a leather coat: some gigantic Siberian freezer, turned into a reconditioning camp. At sixty-eight years old, better to plant a bullet in your forehead.

The clever Kireyev had it all planned, as usual, managing to keep all the researchers and tell-tales away from our nightly overtime work. By this stage, their attention was entirely focused on Konstantin and Boni, whom they never left out of their sight; they wouldn't even notice a heart attack in their own chests, such was their obsession with counting each and every breath of those two.

Grafting Karakurt's visor wasn't easy; we were forced to employ a raw prototype, developed at the Balapan Bunker, certainly not the device destined to be fitted to Konstantin—which had already been assembled and machine-tested. We couldn't do any differently.

The visor consists of two main elements: a multi-mirror lens—back in the Bunker, specialized engineers managed to miniaturize some of our spy satellites' sensors—meant to convert images into digital signals, and an embryonal chemical energy transformer capable of interacting with the cells of the subject's inferior temporal gyrus. What the instruments suggested, after we'd tested the functionalities of the newly-configured visor, exceeded our expectations, despite it being only a prototype. Though it couldn't guarantee fluidity in the process of image acquisition and interpolation, it was the best we could do in the short time available. Rhabdomancy and luck, and some other ingredient with the neutral taste of chance.

Of course, we didn't have time to study and consider the possible effects on memory of this neural-electronic mediation with the IT cortex, but that seemed secondary. What mattered, in the short term, was to reach an acceptable result in visual perception, in terms of image recognition: faces, differences in shapes and colors and between backgrounds and subjects; in short, everything that could grant a basic functionality of the comprehension matrix of the physical world.

The grafting procedure lasted four hours, last night, and this time the bastard took point; after the scalpel job, he sutured, humming a Puccini air (surprise!), then he straightened his back, breathed deeply through his nose, then puffed out all his arrogance: *Here we are, Pavel. See? It wasn't impossible.*

But his Karakurt is still under. We can't know if that device, grafted on the subject's forehead (after surgical removal of his eyeballs), making him look like a twentieth century's techno-cyclops, will really work; and for how long.

Konstantin is in good shape; he's almost ready for the final field-test. His neck gills (no new gills have appeared) had some issues, caused by the low humidity of the environment he's confined in. Nothing serious, simple infections resolved in a few days. We've reconfigured all the settings of his small lair, increasing its similarity to a chunk of Earth-2 might be, after the big bang of the Green Apocalypse.

In a few days (we're slightly late, thanks to Karakurt's visor) we'll move him into the radiation blast, the simulator delivered to us—all smooth and set—from the Kapustin Yar base. If he survives that portable radioactive furnace, as we fully expect him to do, we'll be able to say that we made it, that Prometheus is born...or resurrected, based on your perspective on things.

The mutation protocol will be standardized for mass production... But at that point, Kireyev will have frozen me out already (as I write this, I check my neck with my fingers—still there), just in time to sign and protocol all the papers, and wear his best suit for the private party at the Kremlin. While, on the Red Square, they'll be already setting up the performance which they'll feed to the citizens: the Soviet Prometheus parading as he rides the blast, an item so alien as to impress everybody—Americans included.

But what really matters, in this whole story, is to find a solution for Boni. I'll never leave her in that bastard's hands, cannon fodder for his new meaningless experiments. That's the only reason I revealed all my research to him, shared it, securing to his tarry hair the laurel wreath of one of the greatest scientific breakthroughs in human history.

It was only for her, my white peach. *What else would I have left, otherwise?* Lada's ghost drowning every night in her boiling pool, her white skull coming up and sinking again without end, like a buoy of anguish; or Klara's shadow, walking by the Moskva shores, throwing bundles of memories in the water until they dry out and deflate like a holed balloon; or my bloodied hands? *Only this poison, nothing else?*

I don't have the right teeth for honors and similar shiny trinkets, the bastard can keep them…he'll be able to polish them, use them as mirrors for his warped ego… What I need is to bite something that can fill this hole inside me, behind the valve of my navel. Yes, this is my treatment for Loneliness…that plague that scratches inside, and there's no other cure for this infection, if not the impudent smile of the girl from Kiev, who appeared in the Bunker tunnels like a gust of pure oxygen, her orange lips, her bitten nails and that will to live (so absolute and armed) floating in her almond eyes…a gas of honey, steppe, hot bedsheets, rain and jazz to breathe deep, that made me wish to live a hundred years more.

Boni is still stable at Level 3. In fact, she's ready for the big leap. I'm tampering data, gaining time to spare her the stress chamber which already cooked Ermil's flesh and turned my young fisherman, Konstantin, into a charming, perfect, probably immortal creature—but with faint traces of humanity left. He's assimilating his new nature, wearing its armor with all the consequences. Mornings spent seeing the dawn and hearing the drag of nets on the Aral's shores will soon be removed from his memory or repositioned in an ancillary area.

I don't want the same thing to happen to Boni, a bride who pirouettes like a kaleidoscopic top, the wide skirt of rays piercing her hips, all the while slipping out of her ribbed corset. Her memories still fixed in those dark eyes, marrying her to the internal combustion of a life always tearing along. The first blackberry picked on tiptoes, then the sidewalks of Kiev where she sits on a cardboard box, staring at a weak polar star, up there, hungry for life, like her. An existence that always knows how to get back on its feet, soaking in spices and market voices and, at the same time, moving in the time-zone of rubles, necessities, human essences bottled up in a whorehouse room, upholstered with naked bodies, red backgrounds and empty eyes (like those watered down with liquid plutonium) of Modigliani's paintings. Cheap copies, like those without pants, nothing else than human carbon paper.

This cannot be lost, nor reduced to limbs of experience drifting in the bottom of a radioactive zero.

Some days ago, I gave her some drawing blocks and tempera colors, so she stopped covering her cell walls with her essential oils (green, orange), long necks and those alien faces in the shape of almonds, too-soon trickled on the floor; gone. Now, Boni has all the colors, and she'll be able to add electricity to those unmoving, lifeless rectangles. I feel exactly like those white sheets of paper.

Kireyev took a bite to his hand, during a gland-exploration visit—and some street insult; now he's more than cautious when approaching Boni. But she doesn't react, instead looking through me as though piercing a crystal shape with no veins, heart, or lungs. What's so interesting on the other side? *Why doesn't she use her teeth on me, too?*

Better those, than feeling nothing, like a white sheet.

Lada used to do the same, when I was sent to the Bunker and entrusted with the little hardheaded girl from Kiev. And every time I'd visit my daughter at home, she insisted, until I agreed—madly—to her treatment; and then she resumed seeing me, talking to me, until the cursed pool immersion—*Don't look at me!* she cried, in the end, while the murderous cocktail I'd prepared was mercilessly flaying her.

Everything is so absurd. I hadn't seen it before, and then, later, I couldn't see.

She didn't want to be any less than Boni… Lada could see my obsession well, while I, at least in the beginning, was blind to myself; maybe, if I had a visor, things would be different today. Even this journal.

Night. Not only did Karakurt wake up without any problem, but he also showed off his excellent health and full functionality by assaulting a guard, tearing his head off, throwing a couple of the technicians into the air, those tasked with the construction of Reactor Zero (that's right: they're also building that down here, among the many lethal delicacies surrounding us; I already see myself enjoying a plutonium 239 tea), and managing to escape from the plant with apparent ease.

After Urgant's "disappearance," no security breach had ever occurred in this secret site. Today, the plant—or better: this huge cylinder-shaped cellar, three hundred meters tall, above which the atomic cathedral par excellence will soon rise—seemed as leaky as a sieve. But I'm sure Kireyev was behind that, too: the alpha moth, the saboteur. The bastard had keys for his pet's cage, and he wouldn't certainly hesitate to set up a fake escape—with a few heads rolling from among the highly expendable human material sharing this underground life (that doesn't exist) with us.

He fooled me once again, bloodying my hands. *Accessories' hands are just as dirty.*

He's freed his Karakurt, his idea all along, forget reassignment and temporary tasks. That mutated assassin had already been condemned to obliteration by the Kremlin; and that would have been a very good thing.

MARCH 11, 1965
VLADIMIR IL'IČ LENIN NUCLEAR PLANT, ČERNOBYL'
UNIT ZERO – ACCOMMODATIONS 3B

Morning. Kireyev came to my room again, and he warned me to keep my mouth shut about Karakurt—the visor and all the rest.

General Semerov will be here at the plant in the afternoon for an emergency meeting. The two of us will be the targets of many uncomfortable questions. *Pavel, beware of what you say…the girl would be involved, too. We don't want that to happen, no? You just need to keep your temper.* His words stuck.

It's "in or out," he repeated—not only about the project. The Kremlin is pretty shaken, apparently...even the bastard's bureaucrat friends seem to have lost their cynical aplomb. Karakurt's actions—currently wandering out of control in the area around the plant—are heating up a lot of chairs.

Two weeks have passed since the assassin "escaped" the complex (unsteady official version), and within a range of thirty kilometers from our spontaneous grave in the technologic Hole, a lot of "accidents" have happened. Not a pretty word, especially when coming out of a Soviet mouth. The atmosphere, upstairs, is already jumpy over the massive American bombings—by now systematic—in North Vietnam, and what's happening here may precipitate things.

Not many news about what's happening around the world, reaches the Hole unless it is sporadic and propaganda-driven. But at least once a month, I can count, on my personal *Radio Londres*: old Ozram. He told me about the recent Viet Cong attack against American air force installations at Pleiku, and about the Yankees' muscular retaliation—as good as Nazi-German bomb runs. We did our part, restocking the harbor of Haiphong with armaments, and the tension is now extreme. I wanted to know more, but before long my crazy friend unplugged his contemporary history, to offer up his most recent inter-curtain musical discoveries. The last song I listened to on the phone was Bob Dylan's *The Times They Are A'Changin'*, a perfectly fit for my current situation. Hell, strong stuff.

But Ozram isn't totally crazy: he gets how things work. All our phone calls are controlled, obviously recorded, and yet nobody has ever reported us. It's nothing serious, just music after all—though stars and stripes—but propaganda officials should surely have intervened by now, formally reproaching me and suspending my communications with the outside until a later date.

So, the key to this link—which reassures me that I'm still alive, though buried—must be a passion for music, or mere curiosity, on the part of the two KGB operators tasked with snooping on my phone calls. Ozram must have guessed right away because he always mixes up the information—eking it out—with his clandestine soundtrack. Perhaps, those guys dance, sealed like salted codfish inside their armored post, enjoying a few minutes of enemy rock 'n' roll.

But the current news, here in the guts of the plant and its half-colonized area—a circle thirty or forty kilometers in range—has all the markings of Karakurt's blue face. He's the first-page monster of this microcosm, wedged in Europe's widest swamp, with a big hole in the middle and a pot-bellied subterranean atomic cathedral playing the dim star and letting things orbit around it in tight ellipses. Frozen villages, dirty roads, unmapped military-controlled areas, armored warehouses crowded with flies, sculptures, and top-secret cabinets, black grass, and the dark wallpaper of the stern industrial facilities of Chernobyl. And then the wind-swept forest, with its mouth shut until some days ago. Before the screams.

No newspaper articles; instead the news comes to us directly, printed in dried-blood ink: pairs of cut-off heads abandoned (almost every day) in front of the hidden entrance of the plant, like provisions of fear. Karakurt is raiding the surroundings: Denisovich, Polesskoe, Chistogalovka, Old-Shepelichy, Trubovschina, Stechanka, Rud'ko, Retchitsa…those still-screaming faces come from villages-turned-hunting grounds; and people, in line at police stations and then on the squares, in front of tiny churches—as always gathering the moods of the humble— cry out all their rage, so much so it requires the intervention of a Red Army contingent to restore order.

They're just few souls, of course, we're definitely not on the outskirts of Mexico City…but the brutality of the murders has spread rumor and disorder. Soon, even the gagged Soviet media will have to say or write something. The bureaucrats' embarrassment—the ones financing Project Prometheus since Day One—is at its apex.

Our atomic demon moves quickly across the area, and he plays rough. He must eat and—as we sadly learned with the victims of the abnormal legion, pulverized in the Bunker—the human brain is the main ingredient in his mutant diet.

Kireyev has good reasons to fear the visit of the General and his goons, and I'm risking a lot, too. *Accessories' hands are just as red.*

I must tell the facts. Distance myself.

Night. I can but lie awake after what happened.

I'm not even sure I'm still alive, and the azure light of my room makes my eyes burn.

Semerov blew in like a fury and he cleaned up. This time, one of the bureaucrats was with him (very bad sign), one of the nameless ones—Cuban cigar in his teeth and coat pockets swollen with epuration lists and addresses of re-education centers (maybe, he was one of the diamonds of the dreaded GRU).

Interrogations have been tough, like in war time. When my turn came to enter the room set for the Holy Inquisition, I shuddered. The Torquemada of the day was none other than Rostok, his tools of the trade in a tidy array on the table in front of the chair waiting for me. He was handing his glass eye, wrapped in a handkerchief, to the nurse. Only the two of them were there—the team of pain. No General, officials, or KGB men.

Couldnnn...n't wait to mm...meet you, Professs...sor. I heard so much abo...about you.

Such was the carnifex's grotesque preamble. I was hearing him talk for the first time. His stammer made the situation even more disturbing; like the scar marking his scalp over the right ear. *Thiii...is? At Vilnius...lonnn...ng ago.* He'd noticed I was staring at that horrible wound, sloppily patched up.

Then, tilting his big head sideways, he reached for a small recorder on his worktable. He pushed the button, summoning a weeping child. That was the symphony meant to accompany all the rest. That's to say, darkness and nothing else. They put a hood on my head (I didn't even think to pull it off, despite the fact that my hands were free); and for over two hours, my senses could reach nothing but that cursed cry, bouncing around the room and in my head. A quick-setting poison.

And then I began perceiving other noises, finally something different, besides my breath and the burning napalm of my thoughts. Rostok was handling something metallic. *What was it?* The son of a bitch wanted me to hear the jaws of the unknown slowly closing around me, waiting for them to suddenly sink in.

A buzzing, soft hands (surely the nurse's) taking off my shoes and slowly pulling down my pants to my ankles, baring my legs. An injection in my arm, through the white coat.

My hands were still free, but I didn't move, at the mercy of Rostok and his fiendish plans. Challenging him? No, I simply hoped to muddle through by passively following every instruction. After all, I wanted to talk. To explain the facts, from Karakurt's visor to everything else, so I shouldn't be so afraid of an interrogation—Kireyev was the true responsible of that slaughter.

But nobody was asking me questions. *Why?*

The buzzing was growing in intensity, I felt Rostok's sinister tool approaching my left thigh, a few millimeters away. Heat, a strong burning stench…something was heating up, ready to work on me. *A miniature buzz-saw?* I was afraid to be flayed and my soft parts removed. I'd heard about that, like many other legends about KGB creative torture. But awareness was coming and going, that cursed cry digging inside into my brain and nestling there…and I didn't know what I'd been injected with. I only remember that the gloom I was immersed in began to take shape, at some point, the child's cry changing voice and tone, and now I was seeing Boni's lips, red, piercing my black sarcophagus. They moved—she was the one singing, now. But I couldn't catch the words. Seconds later, another voice joined hers , Lada's, shriller, quickly modulating and leaping in volume and intensity until she was screaming. The pools… *Don't look at me, don't look at me!* And then silence. Konstantin's hands, marked by mariner knots, squeezing hard on the bars of the immersion cage. All the lights suddenly turned on, like spotlights on the stage, and I was once again in the Bunker, in front of my mutation projections. An injection in my arm, the switch turning everything off again, the Atomic Lake, a shape on the shore, this time not a fisherman looking for sirens, much less a cyclopean myself. A man, wrapped in his white coat, with the Prometheus Project logo printed on it, holding a grinning chopped head under his arm.

There was a lock of white hair, turtle-framed spectacles, a lens snapped off. *Urgant, yes.*

I realized I was sitting on a flat stone looking at him. Then the water rose like a freak wave, hitting me, choking me, a double black skin on my face, soaked and heavy. The last image I remember—in that wigwag of hallucinations and sensations—was about the bastard, Kireyev, playing dice with Karakurt's eyeballs, rolling them on an endless metal table. He wore the visor, while his pet awkwardly hopped around him like a blind hungry dog.

And then nothing else. No questions that I remember.

But they must have gotten the whole story, somehow, if I'm still alive here in my room, and almost whole myself. Inexplicably, no mark or wound on my left thigh (did I really imagine it all?), but watching myself in the mirror, I look ten years older… I'm grey like the walls of this steel box…gray except the twenty centimeters square colored by one of Boni's drawings: a three-breasted young woman, breast-feeding three fat men with tousled white hair. *Customers from another life, probably.*

But this is nothing, compared to what Kireyev must have gone through in Rostok's hands. Considering how things ended up.

An hour ago, I received an unexpected visit, marking a point of no return in this story. Adrianov, the lanky plant director—a mere minion that I've never made much of— informed me that the investigation is closed, and that I'm cleared.

I kept my mouth shut about Rostok's "psychedelic" little service, as I wanted to avoid any more troubles—considering there are no marks or proof of ill-treatment, if not in my head. The sensible thing to do was ending the whole cursed matter there—just as they wanted.

I gave a sigh of relief; but then the director, nervously fixing his tie knot, added to his aseptic spiel: *the project must be considered suspended until further notice.*

I didn't even listen to the other words coming out his mouth, I just saw his thin lips moving.

I needed nothing else, to understand everything.

MARCH 13, 1965
VLADIMIR IL'IČ LENIN NUCLEAR PLANT, ČERNOBYL'
UNIT ZERO

I haven't seen Konstantin and Boni since; I no longer have access to the Safe Zone, and I can move around the complex accompanied only by a camo-suited gorilla. Kireyev has vanished, too. But that was to be expected. *Clean-out in grand style.*

I'm here in my room, sitting on my bed in front of a suitcase full of nothing. They'll come to pick me up momentarily. I'll leave the Hole forever. I'll be going back to Lomonosov empty-handed. *Project suspended.*

Right, all these months' work only to go back to polish my old chair in the professors' room. As if nothing happened. I'll have to resume classes without being able to say a single word about what happened here, about the extraordinary—though inconclusive—results we've achieved, dragging Project Prometheus so close to its final destination. A project that never even existed, now put on ice by the bureaucrats.

Talking about this story (even a hint) would mean joining Kireyev, if he's still alive, in a reconditioning facility...chemically lobotomized, playing chess with old wrecks with mustaches dirtied with dull broth and lumps of melancholy. When they let you out of those places, the treatment over, you don't even look like your old self: you piss your pants and hope that the Dark Lady comes to take you soon.

I don't know how my candidates will end up. If the project has actually been suspended, as they say, they should get rid of them. Obliterate them. But I don't think so. They represent the vanguard of genetics in flesh, bone, and brain (and gills, in Konstantin's case), stuff not even dreamed of by the Yankees; it would be nonsense to turn them off, embalm them, pack them up in black plastic bags and bury them in a cell at one of our top-secret museums of horrors.

But I won't ever know.

What's clear is that the bureaucrats are currently busy conceiving a new strategy to compete against our overseas friends... You hear about that even down here (patriotic technicians' verbal incontinence).

The trendy battlefield is now space. After the last flights of the Vostok/Voschod capsules, which launched the first woman into space, a Soviet woman, we're about to make another killing. Three weeks ago, an arrogant mission was announced—the first extravehicular activity in the history of human space exploration. If everything goes as planned, our glorious fighter-pilot and cosmonaut Leonov—son of a Siberian farmer and horse breeder—will hop on the saddle of his spacecraft, get out that technological knick-knack, and hang in the great absolute void attached to an umbilical of twelve meters. A space stroll... the first. Stuff to make all the drums of propaganda roll.

Will Leonov be the new Prometheus, after all?

Here, instead, in the plant that doesn't exist, everything is pitch black. Every day we collect the remains of Karakurt's grim deeds (why does he bringing his scalps all the way here?), one of the chosen ones in disgrace, Kireyev's atomic alter ego spending the last months of his new existence terrorizing the area's population. Entire army special squads are hunting him down, with no result, despite trained dogs and specialized units with experimental gear able (they say) to pick up the creature's radioactive blood.

But the murders don't stop and every morning, at dawn, strong-stomached personnel are forced to get rid of the perfectly aligned necklace of heads encircling the tree trunks, not far from entrance of the Hole. What exactly is Karakurt's absurd behavior…a challenge? Maybe, his returning here every night to display his macabre collection of beheadings—only meters from his hunters—is just his subconscious wish to be stopped.

But that creature's motivations and his hunt are no longer my business. People has begun calling him "the forest demon." *Surely, by now he has little humanity left.* So, here's what's left of our enlightened project: an enhanced serial killer with disgusting appetites, and two subjects shut in their cells in the Safe Zone, apparently under control, but looked after with growing suspicion. *Potential monsters, too.* Understandable.

I hear synchronous footfalls in the hall—boots—they're coming to take me. All I have to do is detach Boni's drawing from the wall, slip it in my jacket pocket, and put the journal away—before they see it and obliterate that as well. Together with the big fat *zero* I'll be left with, when I get out of here.

I don't think I've got anything else to write.

Ghosts and Windows

April 14, 1970
Moscow

I've just found this journal in the drawer of my study. I remember well the day I left it in there—February 28, 1965—a rainy Sunday; when I'd just got back to Moscow.

Five years have passed. I'd decided to bury it, together with all those cursed memories... *And now? What am I doing with these pages in my hands again?*

I re-read the things I wrote, but so much more was printed in my mind. What I'm holding, here, certainly isn't a transfusion from another time, images and colors... there's too little in here, like seeing old photographs, disjointed scenes sculpting a second among billions; and even putting them all together—a collage—they don't let you taste the pulp of those times. I smelled it, leafed through. It has gathered nothing but dust. These pages are mere husks, and they're infested with nothing.

Just like Lada, here in front of me, confined by her thick silver frame. Fifteen years old, she doesn't know anything yet about pools and K plutonium, and her skin still wraps muscles and skeleton. An odorless husk, with no voice; even her cries would be something. Everything seems dead around me.

And then the other picture, so worn, has always remained inside here. The bookmark of the journal.

I'm rewriting here those words of years ago:

I'm trying to capture, to write down in print, this face before me: fearful, livid, and yet brash…she has always reminded me of Manet's Olympia. Her black bowl cut, her so-white skin, a leather lace tight around her throat with a small aquamarine hanging from it—probably fake.

The mark of her whorehouse, or a customer's gift? Or maybe that stone is her affiliation to the creatures of the Dnepr, holding a few drops of that water impregnated with many stories, billions in every molecule. Her black eyes, like the ink drawing her, sudden holes, bent like the backs of almonds on her pale skin; raised, so proud, by unseen hooks, twin puffs of purple traced by a two-bit eyeliner. Lolita.

And here's what I write today, looking at the same photo, with a heart five years older, letting loose the tentacles of memory, without fear of screwing my thoughts too tight with the bolts of words.

Because, otherwise, I'd be tracing the lines of mere husks again, praising the surface—the velvet of an apricot, the tiny bumps of a lemon—inhabited by nothing, without a belly.

Her angel face sometimes so brash, or fearful and livid like that day in the dimness of a bunker, with the still-fresh hoarfrost of Kiev on her short fur coat. The chameleon image of her continuously changes in my mind, like the seasons, like day and night.

Now, she's looking at me with the spring of a sunny day in Moscow behind her, when Gorky Park raises its green hair toward the Moskva, and the water-sprouts of the fountains draw see-through thighs which keep moving.

Yes, she's everywhere and nowhere; she stands in front of storehouses of images that I've filled through my eyes during the day. All things are just background to her petite figure.

Her black bowl cut, skin like the plate-glass surface of a tropical fish tank drinking the reflection of water plants, mottled with fake emeralds.

Her dark eyes, proud and afraid of having turned into the buttons of an obsession. *Lolita.*

And then the words from 1965. The old ones before and then the new ones, once again; because the girl from Kiev no longer needs to pass from the edges of a printed scene, forced every time to step over and out of her flattened dimension, to sit on my knees and give voice to her thoughts—glued and unmoving inside here, crystallized in chemical black and white—to let them run.

That's when Boni doesn't remain helpless—between the four corners of this by-now dead image; she comes to life, though to my eyes only. She comes out of the rectangle of the photo, with all the budding grace of her petite body, stepping over the impossible, the paper edges and the rubber bands of time, and sits on my knees, grabs my hand, steers it on the pages for a few lines. I let her do it, a sign my loneliness. Here's what she's writing now, through my fingers:

You look at me, what do you see? You cannot see. You cannot really touch me. You cannot know. You cannot feel the saliva on your skin, the cigarette embers, the sweat and wet screams slipping over you like another bed sheet, there in the soldiers' beds.

And then she's gone, every time, letting me fear that she doesn't really exist outside my rotten head, where there's a black hole to be filled every day.

Boni isn't made of paper; she's long since come out of that rectangle. She follows me everywhere, like a curious ghost, walking barefoot, without making a sound. Here she is, beside me. I let her read these lines. She shakes her head, takes the pen, and touches her tongue to the tip. I let her do it, she feels like signing my loneliness after so long. Or maybe strangling it. Here's what she's writing now, again, through my fingers. *Do you see me? You can touch me if you want, swallow me one glass after another*—my skin first, then my flesh and blood—*and know, see everything.*

She doesn't vanish as she used to, and she wears a new blue dress. Now I know she really exists, liquid and solid. Alcohol burning my throat, wraith scented like clean bedsheets, (hot) shiver along my spine—the quick zigzag of a boiling lizard—obsession. Radioactive heroin.

Five years have passed, and I've always left the windows of this flat open (so Boni can come in and out as she pleases), and there's one cut-off head of Klara's in each room: smiling, crying, insulting me, or singing that song— Dionne Warwick's *Anyone Who Had a Heart*—that she wouldn't stop singing just before they transferred me to the Bunker. She'd only heard it a couple of times (Ozram, my old friend, where are you?), and she made up the words.

Just as she does now. Now that she's gone.

She walked along the shores of the Moskva for too long, looking for a small piece of Lada—*water is a trap, sometimes. Sparkling pools and rivers quickly turning; not the same thing, not the same water.* She's in there now, in her grave, flowing toward the Volga highway, and inside another desk drawer I haven't opened in five years. Not that bloated purplish body they showed me for identification.

No, that's not her.

Three ghost women, in here, buried with me. One still alive—*the girl from Kiev... I know her body still breathes somewhere, in a cell with steel walls, or maybe hidden in that forest...Chernobyl, so far away*—and the other two certainly dead...though one sings, smiles and cries with nothing from the neck down, and the other—*my daughter in a bridal dress, who I see floating on the ceiling, right above me…*

A living ghost? Olympia and her sold-off daughters. Chopped heads, all the same, scattered around the house like grim radios without knobs, green liquid carpets…up there, beneath the attic, hanging in midair, a girl with her arms stretched across the surface, a cross of flesh covered in white brocade, the erratic patterns of the virgin tissue of her radioactive-bridal dress. A necklace of plutonium pearls that don't glitter, her eyes closed, make-up of decay.

What am I writing? The truth is, since they dismissed him from Lomonosov, I have too much time to think, and this house holds too many dead things tight in its teeth…it won't let go of me, let me start anew. It keeps chewing: living ghosts, shadows of yesterday and tomorrow, things yet to come, squeezing them even before they can exist, pinning them here, in this halfway place. This is why I always keep my windows open…winter and summer, it doesn't matter, it's the same. It isn't just for Boni, to let my Lolita in, her double body of Moscow, but also to let the dead things out.

The air, though, still smells like a bunker

APRIL 30, 1970
MOSCOW

Yesterday, old Ozram came to visit. He doesn't look any older; time only goes by for me, and so quickly. *Do you believe in guardian angels, stuff like that?* Certainly not me, but if I did, I'd suspect my friend.

I've known him since the year dot, and yet, I realize, I know so little about him. We talk about music and politics, play chess and have a few glasses. But I don't even know where he lives. He appears and vanishes, he's a face, a voice, and a phone number which doesn't show up on any address book.

I know he works for the Ministry of Commerce, so he once said, but he doesn't like to talk about that. He has no family, and sometimes he disappears for weeks at a time.

Another ghost? And, in that case, should he be considered alive or dead?

My imagination runs too wild, especially as I return to these pages, which—like the house—warp things. The magic mirrors of a Luna Park.

And yet I'm the pen. Or maybe not...

Ozram, big and strong like a bear, hugged me tight, then he moved a few inches away to better put me into focus. He looked me in the eye and came out with one of his follies: Look at you, damn, you look like a ghost. A female, that's what you need. Never dropped by the Yaroslavsky? Or maybe you're afraid of losing your nose to the pox?

Then, he proceeded to explain how it works, as though I were a boy. Well, actually, I don't know much about these things, and I'm not interested anyway. But he didn't desist (he appointed himself as a sort of "spirit healer," though definitely aimed at bodily needs) and went into the details. Outside the Yaroslavsky station—or in similar areas— you can read the fees of the whores, who sit with their legs stretched, on the soles of their shoes. Otherwise—he winked, knowing I've always harbored a certain repulsion toward large suburban stations (not for the whores, but for departing trains and some so-typical odors reminding me of death)—he suggested I check out Prospekt Mira metro station. There, I'd find plenty of strolling girls, displaying a rolled-up banknote—three or five rubles in one hand. One green, the other blue.

So the fee is immediately clear, right? No useless chitchat, nobody being fooled, Ozram added with a smirk, as if the oversimplification of such a trade would negate my concerns.

Anyway, he seemed well-informed. Should I be surprised? Of course not—after all, he isn't married, nor has he any intention of dedicating too much of his lifetime (what life is that?) to finding himself a proper companion.

Then, after a couple of glasses of vodka—accompanying a lively argument about the Prague Spring and its cannon-shot epilogue—he pulled out his favorite theme: music. Wait. Whispering, as though he were about to reveal a State secret, he suddenly grew serious, then he got up from the sofa and looked for something in his coat pockets.

Damn, where is it? he groaned repeatedly.

And lo! his secret, such as it was. His usual miniature recorder (I've always wondered how he came to owns a device like that...the stuff they sell at the shops downtown weighs kilos), was bound to contain something new. His latest inter-curtain soundtrack.

He pushed a button, switched on his most revolutionary gaze, and gave voice to that song: *I Can't Quit You Baby*, by Led Zeppelin.

New stuff...he briefly commented, then he raised his index finger in front of his nose, gesturing me to stay quiet. And so I did, with my back glued to the armchair listening to the vibrations of that guitar, so strange, and imagining the words of that story. I don't understand English too well, but some phrases went straight to my brain. The song seemed to talk about a special girl, who messes up someone's life, becoming a flaming desire—something very close to an obsession.

It couldn't be a coincidence. I never told my friend about Boni, about what happened in the Bunker and then in the Hole, at the plant. And yet the song, chosen among thousands by Ozram (is my friend a guardian angel, or the opposite?), summoned back the girl from Kiev, there, close to the window, a few meters from us. It had never happened before when somebody else was present. The music, those electric blues, were guiding her in a slow, sinuous dance, climbing up her legs to her hips, lingering there a few seconds, soft, fluid, then climbing towards her chest, whirling on her small breasts and finally dispersing throughout her entire body like molasses, grace, sensuality. This time, she was completely naked, and the light from the street lamps enveloped her flesh in a tight yellowish wrap. Only I could see her, she was dancing for me.

Now all those stories about the Prospekt Mira girls made sense, with their rolled-up banknotes; three or five rubles, green and blue.

MAY 2, 1970
MOSCOW NIGHT.

Today, another human being besides me was in the house. And it wasn't old Ozram, who's vanished again into his black hole.

Who, then? Black bowl cut, dark eyes, eyelids stained with the azure of a cheap eye-shadow, a leather lace tight around her neck, with a hanging star with three diamonds in its belly—certainly fake.

No, not Boni, no ghosts this time; but something that looked almost like her, a few hours ago, among the fat illusions of street chiaroscuros and the flashes of blinking store-signs, white fists holding green and blue rubles, and a few vodka glasses too many in my stomach to awaken reminiscences and imaginary features.

My guest's name was Violetta. At least, so she said, sniffling, as she sat on the stairs of the metro station; but who knows what her real name is. Later, when she came in— *but where the hell do you live? You'll make me lose two hours… That'll cost you ten rubles*—and began undressing, Boni reappeared close to the window. And then, a few seconds later, Lada popped out by her side.

I saw them from behind, both wearing the same shabby clothes—a blue t-shirt with beads on the shoulders, jeans—which Boni had on back when they brought her to the Bunker. Seeing them like that, dressed as twins, I noticed for the first time how alike they look. Same height and frame, except the hair. In fact, I'd never seen them together.

They began whispering a monotonous tune I'd never heard before, and they kept switching places as though in an odd ballet, without ever turning to look at me.

Kolobok, small and round, Kolobok, going downhill. The wolf opens his mouth. Kolobok, I'll eat you, foolish piece of bread.

No, I'm not a Kolobok, but a hedgehog from Chernobyl!

Kolobok, small and round, rolling down without spines, without dread.

As I looked at those ghosts in a daze, Violetta brought me back to reality with a tug. *Hey, I told you ten rubles. Are you deaf or high? Let me see them…and I'll give you a good time.* The girl's face, despite the harsh and assured tone of her voice, looked fearful and brash at the same time. I had chosen her just for that, for how she'd look at me. I pulled the money from my pocket, gesturing her into the bedroom, to wait for me there—*First door on the left. I'm coming.*

Then, I turned my gaze again to the window; Boni and Lada had vanished, but their voices, braided in that sad lullaby (a hedgehog from Chernobyl? Where was that story coming from?), were playing over in my head.

To make them stop, to gain courage to face Violetta, I hit the bottle again, forgetting that Boni was in there. A liquid addiction, a miniature Dnepr, a chunk of river bottled up at 45°.

I let her back in—inside me; for a while, so she wouldn't need to appear in front of the window or on my knees, grabbing my hand and closing this journal. *Enough now, look at me.* She wouldn't even need to appear on the Ferris wheel at Gorky Park, leaping from one seat to the next. She's in my blood, now.

Violetta was on my bed, without her brassiere, and she was slipping out of her pants, raising her legs. Only then— with more light and her skin free—did I notice the holes in her arms…and then on her feet, too, as she let her shoes fly and roll across the floor. She had a liquid addiction, too, a river (different than mine) flowing inside her.

Enough now, look at me, she told me through her teeth; the same words Boni always whispered in my ear.

So? Make up your mind. Or maybe you just want to touch yourself? Okay for me...

With that lullaby still in my head, and the hedgehog without spines whom I pictured still rolling downhill, to infinity—feeling anguished that the creature never reached its destination whatever it might be (perhaps, at the end, it would fall down the Hole)—I closed my eyes for a moment and took a good breath.

I unbuttoned my shirt blindly, then I reopened my eyes and Violetta was still there...but her skin, painted in yellow and orange by the neon sign of the flower shop on the corner, began covering itself with spines.

I'd drunk too much, and that vision turned me into a granite slab. Losing patience, she got up with a snort, approached and grabbed my hand to guide me on the bed, beginning to rub herself against my naked chest. Her spines hurt. Trying to push her away, I kicked, and she fell on the floor. *Hey, what's your fucking issue?*

She dressed hastily and escaped, slamming the door.

I stayed there staring at the ceiling, but nothing appeared up there, not this time. Only a smooth surface with nothing to say or show to me, except a humidity stain in a corner. Lada couldn't float in a puddle so small and dry, surely, she was swimming in another room, and I only perceived her voice—and Boni's in countermelody—as it kept rolling down an infinite downhill, together with the Kolobok, dodging hungry wolves.

MAY 7, 1970
MOSCOW

Violetta was back, yesterday, just after dawn; too soon.

She knocked at my door with all her strength, forcing me to let her in, before the neighbors came out of their lairs to catch something to tell around and slice up my reputation—already at its lowest.

That's why they laid him off, at Lomonosov...the Professor fools around with young girls...

His trash bag is always full of empty bottles...

I can almost hear them already honking, their eyes all bloodshot. They have relatives and friends, ready to take up a nice C-class flat; maybe this building isn't top of the line, especially for a chair-less professor, but it's not that bad either... Well, it used to be more than adequate, until my ghost women began bossing me around in here, turning on and off like light bulbs. But maybe I should simply drink less. Or get away for a bit.

Violetta faced me head-on, her eyes watered down with heroin, or similar stuff giving her the courage to cross Moscow to come here.

I know who you are, Professor... Do you see these? She showed me a shiner and bruises on her neck. She pushed me backward and blew into the flat, marching toward the sitting-room window. That window. Then she turned around, crossed her arms and talked nonsense in a staggering voice.

A hundred rubles, here and now, or else I'm reporting you... You really hurt me, Professor.

All clear. I hadn't even brushed her face the other night (she'd fallen, sure, but a face beaten-up like that...): she just needed money to get high, and she was accusing me for that thrashing. She wanted to monetize what her pimp had done to her, or maybe some other rough customer—more difficult to threaten than me, not without being smacked some more.

While me, I struck her as soft as a cream puff, barely protected by a frail, thin crust. And then again, it was clear that an alcoholic might have memory blanks. Nice move, Violetta. With a face swollen like that, she'd missing a few days' work; some things, you learn on the street, not in a cutting-edge lab, or running after old Lomonosov windpipes. She was a tiger; me, a simple piece of meat, already deboned.

I paid without hesitation, even though I knew the risk—becoming a small bank for that rascal. She'd be back, asking for more money, and then again. *Isn't it how it works?*

But she didn't leave right away, as I imagined, to go to rent a clump of paradise with my money. After slipping the two fifties into her pocket, purplish like her bruises, she smiled, uneasy. She was probably expecting more opposition. So, still standing in front of me, she slipped her red t-shirt over her head (the Tour Eiffel was printed on it. *Had she been to Paris?* What was her story?), she fumbled with the clips behind her back, her shoulder muscles tensing—yes, she was petite, like Boni, but her body was a bundle of sinews set in the right, tender shapes—and she let her bra drop on the floor.

Good, Professor: you earned yourself an extra performance. You can touch them if you want, she whispered, quickly changing her expression.

She'd been a tiger a few seconds earlier, and now she seemed a languid siren with psychedelic eyes. She was both at the same time. She was ascent and descent, and in that stretch of time, finding yourself on the saddle of the summit just before the change, she squeezed your stomach in a vise, pleasant and unpleasant. Both, again. But it was a strong, very strong sensation, like being pressed against an airplane seat during take-off. *Eddies.*

For me—a man who'd buried his emotions in a drawer, in this journal—the effect couldn't help but be tripled.

Violetta's apricot breasts, with their small tobacco-colored buttons, free and aimed at me, awakened the room and my hallucinations. I felt hands squeezing my neck. I couldn't see anything, but I recognized that scent of still alive ghost… Boni, her, her essence of honey and mango; the thin, piercing tropical rain of her adrenaline out of control.

The empty vodka bottle (at five in the morning, already) on the counter, the floor gurgling like the sparkling pools of the Bunker, slowly stripping the flesh off my feet and calves, Boni and Lada on the table playing at tossing Professor Urgant's cold head to one another… Violetta, next to the window, turning her head to either side in jerks, as though trying to adjust to the visor screwed to her visage, under her forehead—Karakurt with tits…

That warped world seemed so real, intense; I could go on writing about it for hours, counting all the absurdities appearing to me in a few minutes, maybe even seconds… but it would be useless, and that's not the point.

When everything finally vanished, I found myself on the floor, exhausted, with my mouth dry and my knuckles bloodied. *No, not like that…*I thought, getting up and struggling to move toward the window. But what I feared, as I noticed the girl's body, began screaming in all its horrid, impossible reality.

Violetta was sprawled on the floor, fainted (so I hoped). I had hit that graceful face—for real, this time—which now, in its deformation of pain, of blood old and new, had a broken, misaligned jaw, and a look of surprise thickly trickling from her nose. I knelt and laid my head on her chest—on her apricot breasts—to check if that heart was still functioning.

Was it still beating? Perhaps. But who could say that in such a state… I was drunk, afraid, disoriented. I was a monster, and of the worst kind.

Overcome with by devastation, before hitting the bottle again (I needed that, my head was screaming) I managed to call Ozram… Luckily, this time my guardian angel hadn't vanished down one of his black holes.

Don't touch anything, I'm coming right away.

OCTOBER 11, 1971
ST. SOPHIA CLINIC – KIEV

Violetta…the last thing I wrote about that morning, about those absurd days. It wasn't easy, choosing to reopen this journal after what happened. Old Ozram forced me to do it, finding it and tossing it on my bed—*get to work, it'll keep you in touch with reality, this time*—and the doctors, too, here at St. Sophia Clinic (in Kiev, Dnipro district, where Boni grew up: a coincidence) where I've been an in-patient for over a year. They consider it an excellent support to rehabilitation, and to the treatment I'm undergoing. Yes, now I'm the guinea pig, just like my super-soldier candidates at the Bunker, and then in the Hole.

No, I'm not in a madhouse, though I risked that. After almost beating poor Violetta to death (she's okay now, under treatment for her drug addiction), I could have ended up at the Scientific Institute for the Criminally Insane Serbskij, hunting ground for that shady character, professor Lunc, always in KGB colonel uniform and perennially looking for crazy brains and dissidents to slice up. My fate would have been very different—compulsory psychiatry, the Soviet way—if not for my guardian angel fixing things.

Nervous breakdown—the "mild" diagnosis they wrote on my chart. *And those hallucinations, my living and dead ghosts?* Nothing unusual: they say that's pretty common for people in my condition. Then, I did my part, gulping down one bottle after another (the only way I knew to stop the enormities echoing in my head).

I haven't touched alcohol since I came here, and the ghosts (of all kinds) never reappeared. Walls and ceilings of this blocky complex are firm, like those of the old Balapan Bunker, but nothing more than they're supposed to be; they don't turn into sparkling pools or bends of inexistent rivers. Nobody can float or swim across this concrete.

Good, but why am I still here, after all this time?

No, there are no ghosts in here; these days they only show up in dreams, stark in-front-of-the-windows of nightmares. Nothing more. Friendly shapes and cursed outlines, misshapen; a hellish theater walled up alive in my head.

They won't come out anymore, Ozram always repeats. *They're fucked now.*

Not even monsters in flesh and bone, along these clean white halls, but I've met somebody who saw them—and was admitted here, just like me, in this strange, long (too long) stay clinic.

Actually, I'm no longer sure, after all this time, that I'm not in an asylum; maybe repainted as a modern psychological rehabilitation center. On the fourth floor, where we aren't allowed, those smiling guardians in white coats must be hiding something. Perhaps that's where they seal the screams, the deliria, and the room with the big brain fryer. *Electroshock.*

Rasim, who made doors and windows for thirty years in the village of Rudko, about thirty kilometers from Chernobyl, saw the monsters. And he wasn't dreaming at all.

The old man told me many stories; we have all the time we want here, to waste our breath, read approved books, and organize chess tournaments.

He began at lunch, on a rainy Sunday (we all eat together here, except the in-patients of the fourth floor, the ghosts): wild-eyed, he turned to either side and, reassuring himself that nobody could hear us, started with the Black Volga. He told me he'd often seen it passing his village, that evil limousine with no plates, with the devil at the wheel and a trunk stuffed with tied-up, gagged-up girls, meant to become sex toys for Soviet bureaucrats; or with redcheeked children, their organs ready to be removed and sold to the best Arab or Western bidder. Just an old urban legend. That was when—listening to Rasim's ravings—I began to suspect that St. Sophia might be something more than a rehabilitation clinic. That old man, though funny, really sounded out of his mind.

Another time, he confided that he'd listened (*with my own ears!* he said, as he pointed his index finger to the middle of his brow) to the recordings of Hell, the cries of the damned recorded by the elusive Doctor Azakov (*who didn't believe in the Bible, but looked for Hell*). A microphone linked to an endless cable had been lowered into the Batagaika thermokarst crater (the Yakuts call it "the Gate of Hell"). Siberian rubbish, only believed by children, demented people and, for some rubles, some middlemen (or potbellied holy men) accompanying small groups of curious visitors and bands of superstitious widows. With an hour-ticket for the netherworld in their teeth, they offer them a Dantesque experience right on the edge of the fissure. *Listen!*

But then, one day, Rasim took me aside in the hall of the first-floor common area, next to the TV room. He grew serious, squeezed my arm, and asked if I could keep a secret.

Professor Todorov, do I have your word?

Considering my history in top secret projects, I'm no longer allowed to use my real surname. At the clinic, I am registered as Todorov, former professor of Modern History, widower, with no children. My new personal profile, made up by the KGB and complete with detailed fake papers. Should I say a word about Project Prometheus, Unit Zero and the underground reactor at the plant (they've actually begun to build it, now), about who I really am? Would I end up in the hands of the Rostok of the day again…and surely it would go worse than last time. Just the thought of it, and once again I hear that child's desperate cry, the favorite symphony of the scientist-butcher with the glass eye.

I'm not afraid of telling the truth—or dying; that's not the point. I just want to hold on to the possibility, though a remote one, of seeing Boni again someday.

But Rasim, as all madmen, manages to perceive things invisible to most. Sometimes, it seems he can read my eyes. If that's the case, he must have seen quite a lot of interesting things.

I gave him my word, and the old man told me another of his stories. But this time, after just a few words, rather than entertaining me as usual, he summoned shivers that crept up my spine.

A blue-skinned demon, with a single red eye, in my garden…

So he began, and a detailed account followed of that chilling experience, dating back just six months ago. I immediately understood it wasn't his usual cheap rubbish, understood whom he was talking about; his demon really existed, had a name: Karakurt.

It had to be him. *But how?* Our "wrong Prometheus" couldn't have survived for so long. Considering his mutated DNA deterioration, which I'd studied extensively with Kireyev, who wouldn't accept the evidence (it's always hard to accept that must lose a child, even a special adopted child like that), and the rejection of his tissue regeneration trait, Boris/Karakurt should have been long since gone. In these past years—between my waking hours and hallucinations—I often imagined him buried under an oak, in that forest around the Hole, his visor turned on over a rock like a perpetual light.

Everything added up. Rasim told me that the creature, hiding in the garden behind his house, had suddenly leapt out to grab his daughter Amina (the mother was from Bosnia) by her legs, dragging her away. He'd seen it all from the window, his hair standing on end (as he told this, he ran a hand through gray tufts, lifting a bundle); shouldering his shotgun, he'd rushed out to chase that cursed beast. But it was late evening, and the demon had escaped, quickly vanishing into the gloom of the woods with its prey.

That was the last time he'd seen his daughter; seventeen years gone in the darkness, but I believed I knew well the destiny of that young head, and of its intelligent, tender contents. But to the poor man, I said nothing.

Despite that night's scarce light, Rasim gave me a pretty accurate description of the creature, and I had no doubt. But then, with tears in his eyes, he added a small but meaningful detail.

A red eye, just under the forehead, flashing on and off; light blue skin, rough… The moon was high, I saw it well, and then these things on its neck, like fish gills. Quick like…

Gills? Abruptly, I stiffened, and my friend noticed. But he misinterpreted my reaction, muttering something in a grimace.

I'm not shitting you, Professor... I know it sounds crazy, but that beast took my daughter. I swear it's all true.

That demon couldn't be Karakurt...among the subjects still alive back when I left the Hole, only Konstantin had developed gills.

Everything added up, and at the same time nothing at all did. Had my Prometheus escaped the Safe Zone? When, and how? *And what about Boni?*

There are no ghosts, alive or dead, in this clinic. But out there, a little over a hundred kilometers from where I'm sitting right now, apparently, there are.

And they are my ghosts.

OCTOBER 30, 1971
HOTEL RADISSON BLU, KIEV

This morning, I finally left the clinic. The always-reliable Ozram came to pick me up, shocking me: he showed up at the entrance aboard an official-looking, shiny black Volga. *Professor... Todorov, please, come aboard.*

At the window of his room to wave goodbye, Rasim's hair stood on end once again. So theatrical.

I'd never seen Ozram with such a grin plastered on his face (it almost reached his ears). My friend wanted my "liberation" to be in grand style, so he'd rented that gargantuan car, only used by politics and five-star diplomats.

Surely, Ozram wasn't aware of that macabre legend, and there was no devil at the wheel, just him. Although some doubt, at that point, was legitimate.

After all, Lucifer used to be an angel, and more infernal creatures may have followed the same route—the same fall—switching to the other team. Some of them might have worked as guardian angels, back in their training years, before having cherub or seraphim insignia stitched to their shoulders, and they well remember how to do that old job: an excellent cover.

And the black holes where Ozram often vanishes? Does he go to Hell, perhaps rappelling down a rope into the Batagaika fissure...is that the elusive Ministry he works for?

These are thoughts which, should I reveal them to anyone, would take me straight back to my clinic room to be sedated again.

Now I'm in my hotel room, still here in Kiev, and again at the Radisson Blu. My choice, this time, nothing to do with Ozram's schedule. He's too sensible to suggest such bullshit.

All right, I can't say who I really am, I'm just a penniless History teacher, good...and sure as death, from now on I'll have a couple of hounds at my heels, checking my every move. But I can still sleep where I want; and choosing this hotel (will I see Rostok's ghost in the corridor?) is a small rebellion.

My new guardian angels are snarling down there, on the chilly road, in their car hidden by the shadows of a row of trees; they must have already smoked a pack of cigarettes by now and called the Kremlin to update the powers that be.

Now, I just have to think about what to do. *Go back to Moscow, to that cursed flat?* Hardly appealing, especially now that I suspect (a euphemism, considering what I heard) that out there, around the foundations of the new Chernobyl Plant, my Konstantin is on the prowl—and it sounds like he's following in Karakurt's steps. *Is he hunting alone?*

This is the question that's going to torment me all night long.

Woodstock and the Prodigal Son

November 2, 1971
Vladimir Il'ič Lenin nuclear plant, Černobyl'
Unit Zero.

Night. Again in my old accommodations in the Hole, here below the Chernobyl plant, which is beginning to show its surface skeleton. Now the foundations of the structure destined to host Reactor 1 stick out of the ground, while the tree line of massive old trunks has begun to bend, avoiding the intrusive competition from the concrete frameworks and steel cages; so, you can no longer say it doesn't exist. But many other things have changed since my last stay here. The Yankees reached the moon in flesh, bone, and spacesuits (Apollo 11 had our Prometheus Zero bite the dust), and they strolled among craters—though our Luna 9 was the first to land on the lunar crust, back in 1966, in a soft landing with no crash. A matter of cuts to space programs, that's what they say in our parts.

Me, I landed—crashed—about a year later at the St. Sophia's Clinic, in Kiev. Such were my feats. Hats off to the Yankees.

There was also the Woodstock Festival, while inside me the psychedelic guitars of vodka were thrumming non stop, and it was hard for me to listen to anything else. In those days, Ozram looked twenty years younger; with his dyed mustache, he behaved like an idiot. He wore thin necklaces and bright shirts with impossible collars. As a hippy, my guardian angel looked obsolete, out of time—an awkward, tuckered-out Soviet version.

But the Flower Children had come to us, too, just like the Woodstock screamers and the counterculture legions raging everywhere. My friend filled my head and ears with Janis Joplin and Jimi Hendrix music, without knowing— back then—that he was going to increase my ghost dose, always to be kept under strict control.

So many things happened, in the intervening years, but these halls are still the same, just like the personnel who hibernated in this secret underground complex, watching over a nuclear reactor that apparently isn't working to speed yet. They wanted to milk plutonium, but all they do is curse Siberian saints.

The world out there has changed, while so many of us here are trying to dodge the present. They shot President Kennedy; comrade Ho Chi Minh is no longer with us; and the Vietnam war goes on with no meaning, with its Hamburger Hills and nonsense like that to conquer a stream or a hill.

Moons and hills, the Rolling Stones and Neil Armstrong, things built and destroyed as quickly and as cynically, like the Aswan Dam and the break-up of the Beatles, while the black Volga of the elephant Brežnev goes back and forth without ever turning.

The Hole sits outside time, vaccinated against change. I came back here only to barter, certainly not out of fear of playing another game of chess with Rostok: Konstantin's head in exchange for Boni—for the chance to see her one last time. An offer I couldn't refuse. *Would I ever have another chance?*

They were watching me, at the Radisson Blu, just out of the clinic; that much I knew. But after a couple of days spent thinking about what to do with the last chunk of my life—with me hiding vodka bottles and Ozram hot on my heels—the couple of KGB hounds sleeping in the car under my window introduced themselves. Semerov, the arrogant and medaled general, wanted to meet me with extreme urgency.

Turns out Rasim wasn't lying; the old man's sight was still good.

There is a Karakurt on the loose, though it is no longer Boris—who, didn't "break down" as quickly as we predicted.

The problem now is—has been for the last two years, actually—Konstantin.

The original Karakurt—Boris—survived well beyond expectations; our projections proved completely wrong. More than two years after I'd left the plant, the monster, the next-gen head-hunter, was still haunting the area, claiming many victims. Special forces intervened more than once, sweeping the area as though looking for a Nazi party official, but all to no avail. Kireyev had done a good job, managing to forge an invincible creature; his Karakurt rose to the occasion, although operating in a standard environment, and not in a high-radiation one. Too bad he wasn't wearing the Red Army uniform and that he would snap off several Soviet heads a day.

A never-ending field-test.

Yesterday, after a friendly pat on my back and a slurred, optimistic *Welcome back, Professor*, I had a rich breakfast with General Semerov. Then, he offered me the opportunity to re-enter the project to help solve the "Karakurt Crisis." In exchange, they promised that I'd be reinstated at Lomonosov; back teaching, and with double the salary. Basically, they asked me to act as bait, to lure Konstantin into a trap, so a squad of elite forces could obliterate him.

You have an ascendancy over that creature...its still-human part, I mean. It'll trust you.

Konstantin had been freed from the Safe Zone in order to eliminate Karakurt, and he single-handedly accomplished the mission where all those special troops had failed.

In two weeks, the monster's head had been delivered, placed next to the massive entry hatch of the Hole, complete with the makeshift visor installed by Kireyev and me.

But Konstantin—having fulfilled his task—was gone.

He went rogue, just like his predecessor, and the homicides resumed with the usual grim regularity. Apparently, despite the great differences in the two subjects' mutations, the human brain is common ground for them. Their feeding needs match, a standard linked to DNA alterations caused by K liquid plutonium, as already observed during the slaughter perpetrated by the abnormals in the Bunker tunnels.

The General's words buzzed in my head like bloodthirsty mosquitoes; he was asking me to put my life at stake, that much I was sure, but I had to accept and face Konstantin, out there, among the roots of the forest. Flush out my Prometheus, look at him in his electronic eye, trick him, and witness his execution. From the moment of his atomic birth (I've always imagined extracting that boy, with my hands and radioactive forceps, out of the uterus of his old life) to his death: come full circle. *Drowning him in his Aral.*

In any case, it's the only way for me to see Boni again.

Otherwise, my life doesn't make sense. I'm drinking again, and going back to Moscow, to that house, would mean restarting my creative factory of ghosts, losing control again and ending up—this time forever—in an actual madhouse. *Electroshock.*

So be it, let's go hunting Karakurt.

November 3, 1971
Černobyl' – Exclusion Zone
First Day of the Hunt

We left just after sunset, the first day of the hunt. I walked, a flashlight in my hand, followed by ten snipers, armed to their teeth and camouflaged with vegetation. Silent, melted into the shadows and the chiaroscuros that the moon (with its stiff and unnatural American flag stuck in her navel) generously spilling onto this killing ground: buckets full of glowing milk.

I chose to go deep into the woods; I was certain it would be the right place to meet Konstantin. *He would find me.*

It was as cold as Hell, and I'd refused to wear adequate military equipment. My old coat, hanging at the clinic without a master for so many months, had to be enough. I was back in it now, and I wouldn't look suspicious to Konstatin dressed that way; but I wasn't sure how long I could endure such temperature, with only a few newspaper pages wrapped about my chest to counter the cold.

I'd accepted a pair of gloves, which didn't look standard military issue, and a funny-looking ladies' kupanka in brown fox fur, borrowed from Semerov. He'd probably used it one the morning after confiscating it from one of his mistresses, to keep ears and brain warm during an outing on his personal game preserve, only a hundred kilometers from here.

The cold had taken him by surprise was how he justified such an odd outfit; I imagined his lover—this week's—forced to accompany him on elk hunts in the woods, with a wailing entourage of Laika dogs, her scalp freezing in order to preserve the General's noble skull. The bureaucrats must have left him without an escort, there at his dacha; by now, he's lost a good part of his support. He's moved dangerously down on the list, and I'm actually a little surprised he isn't already in a reconditioning center, after the mess with the first

Karakurt…though he acts so confident, the dear General must know well he's walking on very thin ice, and that he must hurry.

So much so that, in order to meet me (and persuade me) as soon as possible, he reached the Hole by helicopter directly from his dacha, dressed like that, without taking the time to don his uniform. He showed up with that thing on his head, and a massive short-fur astrakhan on his shoulders, all shiny and probably costing a whole herd of karakul their lives.

With that absurd kupanka on my head, smelling like violets, I walked several kilometers, too many for my scarcely trained legs, going deeper and deeper into the forest. With the flashlight in my hand, I'd be an easy target for Konstantin, should he want to get even with me (I hadn't exactly been the best stepfather). But at the same time, if his intentions were less hostile, and his belly already sated with his disgusting delicacies, he could easily spot me and approach. *The prodigal son.*

I walked until three in the morning, finding only sharp cold creeping in everywhere, and invisible animals scuttling into their lairs through the bushes, troubled by my noisy footfalls and very badly sung songs from Bob Dylan to the Rolling Stones, then fixing on Joe Cocker— *Something*—making up the lyrics to pass the time, and to let Konstantin hear. (Should Ozram hear my shoddy assassination attempts at his holy musical pantheon, his hair would stand on end like old Rasim's.)

Finally, worn out and frozen, I've been forced to return to the base, together with my escort—stagnant in the darkness.

We'll try again tomorrow, perhaps moving more northward.

I'm warm now. Even the Hole has its advantages, after all, and then again…in the Safe Zone, two levels below me, she's there: Boni. I don't know what I'm going to dream tonight, but I think the girl from Kiev will visit me somehow—if she managed to project her ghost-body up to Moscow, reaching me here will be child's play. *How much has she changed?* Maybe she has a portrait of me, hanging in her cell?

A glass of vodka (two, perhaps) is what I need, before lying down and discovering what awaits me.

A toast to your good health, Konstantin! So to speak…

NOVEMBER 4, 1971
ČERNOBYL' – EXCLUSION ZONE
SECOND DAY OF THE HUNT

Today's schedule changed on a moment's notice: though Konstantin hadn't showed up yesterday in the forest—not to us, at least—we were informed about a sighting at the village of Stechanka, about twenty kilometers from here.

Apparently, this time Karakurt had an unfortunate dinner date, and he took some buckshot from a sprightly pig farmer. Was it true? By now, stories about the Chernobyl monster are legion around here. At the base, they hear of ten sightings a day, at least.

But it was different this time: the old man who called the crisis unit (a dedicated phone number has long been in place) gave a detailed description of the creature, and he sounded reliable. In previous instances, as I read in the reports, Karakurt sightings gave diverse and nonsensical appearances: a three-meter tall man, or one with two heads; once, even snake-like.

It's understandable; people are afraid, there have been too many dead…and too many grim remains left over an ever-widening range.

So, in the late afternoon, I climbed aboard a jeep with the cleaners, and we moved toward the area of the sighting; the hunt began with a circular approach, about three kilometers from Stechanka.

With that flashlight in my hand again (initially turned off, as we mobilized before sunset this time), the violet-scented ladies' hat, and a Geiger counter in my pocket, I walked four kilometers, dragging my feet over dry leaves, crossing barren fields, weaving canals, and skittering on frozen puddles. I was thinking after this I couldn't endure another hunting day of hunting. I'd have to give up, would probably find myself in Rostok's toy room. I needed luck, this time.

I reached a yellowing farmhouse, which looked deserted, and I diverted from our pre-planned spiraling path, meant to lead us to the first houses in a few hours. The soldiers shadowing me couldn't object to my change of plan, as they weren't allowed to show themselves. The radio hanging from my belt flashed, warning me that I'd taken the wrong direction; but it was two in the morning already, and I wanted to try my luck. I would have done anything to keep from wandering in circles across those fields.

And yet, I used to attract ghosts like honey… I didn't even have to move from my bed. They were always there, everywhere, arcane windows and watery ceilings, doors on parallel realities ready to show me those dancing lunacies, evoked by my broken emotions.

But apparently, Konstantin's story was different (in fact, he never showed up in my hallucinations), though I was sure he'd spotted me; he knew where I was, constantly, following me most of the time, challenging my armed escort.

Slowly, I closed in on that isolated building, and a light suddenly turned on and off inside it. Nothing else, no noise. It looked like an invitation.

The door was closed, and the animated light bulb had shown me, through a window with no panes, a blurry movement, almost imperceptible…a figure that must have shifted, very quickly, across the room on the far side of the entrance, and a beaten porch.

I stopped—as though waiting for something—a few meters from the arches supporting the upper floor, holed by three large wooden windows; just a step from the narrow black tongue of floor they hid, with a short double door looming in the middle. *Was I still relying on my rhabdomancy to map the invisible?* It was all so absurd that anything, any thought, could be justified.

Then I heard a voice—Konstantin's, I couldn't be wrong, though it sounded hoarser than I remembered. *You may come in, Professor. But please, warn your friends to stay put...we'll be just a few minutes.* Just as I thought, I hadn't found him out of mere luck or thanks to my bright intuition. He'd been waiting for me, had chosen to meet me right there, in that sick farmhouse which had drawn me like a magnet.

I turned for a second toward a tight row of bushes, bordering a meager road grooved by knobby tractor wheels. The cleaners must be there, ready to leap out and surround the building. I raised and moved my arm, as though repeatedly pushing a car horn in the darkness, to ask them to wait, to give me time before unleashing Hell. *Would they understand? And in that case, would they listen?*

Maybe I was asking too much of those soldiers; they were all wound up and would struggle to hold back. The smallest spark would be enough to give life to their flame throwers, and all the rest. My thoughts were feverish. I knew one of them had lost a sister, years ago, to Karakurt. It had been Boris to crash her skull, but that didn't make any difference.

A monster is a monster, and someone must pay.

My small radio was still flashing, so I grabbed it and communicated with Sergeant Korelev. He could keep his men at bay, at least for the few minutes Konstantin had asked for.

Five minutes, Professor, maybe... The boys chomp at the bit, here, I can't guarantee anything. His warped voice croaked. I couldn't squeeze out any more time, so I groped my way to the double door, suddenly blinded by the light turning on (so white) under the porch. I felt naked, maybe dead too. But nothing had happened, everything going to Konstantin's plan.

After a deep breath, I pushed the door open and tiptoed in. He was there, sitting before a rough wooden table. There was a half-empty vodka bottle on it, a loaf of bread, and two chopped heads, with their skulls open and thoroughly emptied. No blood; everything had happened hours before. One head looked smaller than the other, but maybe the long red hair of the other victim, tricking my eye on the proportions.

A man and a woman? Or maybe a woman and a kid, her son?

I couldn't keep my eyes on that abomination any longer, fortuitous because Konstantin's voice made my head jerk up.

I've been waiting for you, Professor. All things must come full circle, no? His words made my blood run cold. Full circle. Yes, that was exactly what had been in my head since leaving the clinic.

I needed a drink, my hands were trembling with anguish, and once again Konstantin read my thoughts, offering me a glass and inviting me to sit before him.

Those two poor heads divided us, like the still life of a drunk Picasso, making our reunion unnerving and grotesque. Silence…a wasted minute. *Were we going to cast a die to decide who would speak first? Who would come full circle?*

He stared at me as though I were some extinct reptile stripped from the fossil clay of the Mesozoic, and magically brought back to life with a glittering tail and a brand-new livery. Had he thought me dead?

He'd changed. Besides the visor that had been grafted to his face, his skull had stretched and grown; while his skin, still blue, now showed silver streaks, branching raylike from his nipples, and it looked thicker and tougher… And then, on both sides of his ribcage, another pair of gills vibrated in sync, twins of those on his neck.

His mutation had surely gone further, but I couldn't observe more. His chest was bare, but he wore camo pants and combat boots.

Three minutes. I felt the adrenaline of the snipers flowing, out there in the dark, like a newborn boiling torrent. The castanets of their triggers would soon begin their clicking dance. Worriedly, I checked the window to my left; Hell was to come that way. My fallen Prometheus was quiet, unfazed by the situation. He was surrounded, he wouldn't make it out this time.

But that was what he wanted; he'd walked into that trap on purpose.

Why?

We were short on time; the fourth minute was dangerously close to dying. He followed my quivering gaze, going back and forth from his face to the window and the fields shot with ink which seemed to tighten more and more around the farmhouse, like giant hoses of black rubber.

Then, finally, he made up his mind, and revealed how we would come full circle. His words, harsh and mournful, left no doubts; at that point, it was what I expected, assuming the story made any sense.

It's like heroin, he began, almost whispering, caressing one of the smooth cut-off heads on the table, then turning that dead, spirited face, and its vacant skull dome toward me. A woman, with no brain nor future. Red hair, a dead plant attached to a bulb of flesh torn from the soil of her body.

I know it seems horrible, but it makes your heart thrum and there's no other way to feel alive with this plutonium blood freezing inside you... You know what I'm talking about, it was you pumping it into me. But then their swallowed memories, chewed memories...they survive, go stale inside, become voices, hundreds of them, and they make you insane. In a few minutes this woman, too, will tell me her life, from the beginning to the end, and then the other way around. Make them stop, Professor. Come full circle. You must do it.

This is what I remember, at least, as my head was functioning intermittently: I was listening in shock. Prometheus, before me, handing me a 9mm Makarov, leaning back in his chair, letting his arms drop toward the floor, his head tilted backwards and his mouth open. He wanted the bullet shot straight into his brain. To be healed in a blink of the emotional infection torturing him. Cutting the power was vital to shut up, finally, all those voices. Before the red-haired woman and the kid could join the macabre choir using Konstantin's head as a sound box. *Heroin.*

Five minutes. I shoved the gun barrel into his mouth, pushed it against his palate, and squeezed the trigger. Then, after the shot, the bullet hailstorm from my eager friends came; I threw myself on the floor and waited for the storm to pass under a blanket of glass, my face splattered with Konstantin's burst torments. Prometheus' riddled carcass shook as though electrocuted, before falling from the chair and collapsing, blue and red, a few centimeters from me. Then, I saw his visor shuttering like a bear trap and darkening. It reflected my face.

NOVEMBER 5, 1971
VLADIMIR IL'IČ LENIN NUCLEAR PLANT,
ČERNOBYL' SAFE ZONE NIGHT.

A day I won't easily forget.

Today the plant director, Adrianov-the-Lanky—even thinner now—accompanied me to the Safe Zone, escorted by two bears in camo suit. The General had kept his promise: I got to see Boni before going back to Moscow and Lomonosov.

What should I say to her about Konstantin? I would wing it—there were so many things I wanted to know about her, after so long.

At her cell, I gestured Adrianov to wait a moment before unlocking the heavy hatch and letting me in.

I was a meter away, maybe two, from my obsession. In flesh and bone this time.

From outside, from the narrow corridor running alongside the chosen ones' quarters, I could watch her without being seen, through a wide one-way mirror.

The cell was larger than I remembered, maybe not even the same one, although the walls were covered in drawings. No bodily fluids or biological palettes: they'd kept her stocked with tempera colors and all the tools she needed to stage that small, melancholy art exhibit. She was surrounded by—even sitting on—her anthropomorphic, long-necked figures, with their thin bones and empty sockets, which I'd come to know a long time ago.

The drawing that I took with me to Moscow—the young three-breasted woman breast-feeding three fat men— which had hung on the wall of my clinic room, too, is currently inside this journal, folded in four, together with the picture of the girl from Kiev back when she came to the Bunker; my ghost bookmark.

But now, her new works showed something different. Those alien, elongated figures were set in detailed scenes, no longer monochromatic backgrounds of an empty space—white, black, or red. Men and women, all naked. There were medals on the males' chests, pinned directly on their skin; the others were apparently prostitutes, without breasts or with a black hole in their chests where their hearts should have been. They were in rooms with red walls. One drawing framed, through a window, a watery bend of the Dnepr; another, the largest, portrayed a lab in the background, a wide observation window in the middle, while the greenish waters of a pool with empty floating cages stood in the foreground. One of the immersion pools at the Bunker, no doubt; she could still remember those well. The same was true for me.

While I watched her, she worked frantically on a new drawing: a male figure in white coat, holding a girl with blonde hair braided at her nape, and her purple skin covered in scales.

Was that me with Lada? Was she feeling I was there, close again?

Beside her, on the floor, was another sketch; quick, less detailed than the others, it showed a forest sprayed in red, an angel on the ground with a blue-skinned woman straddling him. *Her? But where?*

The girl from Kiev hadn't changed. Time never touched her harmonious body, covered by smooth azure skin. The perfect lines of her back looked like a stepping stone made of flesh, waiting for the eye of the observer to leap on the golden domes of an imaginary Jerusalem: she, with her curves and alleys, the perfect place where to live and die.

I'd been warned about her refusal to wear any clothes, and that she hadn't uttered a word since my dismissal and my hasty return to Moscow.

Finally, excited, I asked the director to let me into her cell.

As soon as she saw me, she jumped to her feet, moved her lips as though to say something, then bent, grabbing the still-incomplete drawings from the floor and using them to cover her breasts and groin.

*Boni, I'm so happy to…*I said, not knowing how to go on. She shook her head, as though not believing what she was seeing.

Was she afraid of me? Or worse, did she hate me?

It was understandable; after all, I was the one who'd transformed her into a freak-show creature, condemning her then to a meaningless life sentence. But why hadn't she been obliterated, considering the grim deeds of the two Karakurts? They still had to explain that to me. Anyway, she'd never undergone the stress chamber, so she wasn't like Boris and Konstantin; her mutation was still incomplete, on stand-by…but she could suddenly evolve into something different, become dangerous.

After some minutes' uncertainty, she approached, reaching for my face, letting the drawing covering her breast flutter toward the floor. With her fingers, she delicately explored my mouth, nose, jaw, forehead, and hair. Then, her open palm stopped on my heart, lingering there, almost listening.

Her touch was strange; hot, cold, and wet at the same time; within her almost-scorching fingertips, a fitful icy current seemed to flow, which must surely tap some alternate source for its energy.

K liquid plutonium, of course, her radioactive blood vibrating along the electrical cords running through her—double veins and arteries rerouted by her mutated DNA throughout her body, parallel to the old ones.

After a silence swollen with many things, pregnant with vibrations, with the background of the air conditioning leafing through walls of drawings, she rose on tiptoes and whispered something in my ear.

Take me away from here.

Look Homeward, Angel

May 9, 1986
Moscow

Chance and coincidence; I've been dealing with those two for a long time, as much as drip-feeds of vodka, ghosts, and underground holes.

So what's new? Two weeks ago, on April 26, 12:04 am (I've always been good with numbers, less so with women), I turned seventy, and the same day Reactor 4 of the Chernobyl plant exploded. *Boom!*

I almost feel like laughing, thinking back on it…and the bottle works as an amplifier. Me and plutonium, what a couple, arm-and-arm like contaminated bride and groom—it's a silver-colored metal, a sharp son of a bitch, but it's female to me…she seduced me like a boy cumming in his pants in front of a crumpled porno magazine…

I imagine the two of us taking our tainted, malformed children to the Luna Park, attached to the cords of red balloons (their melted shoes hanging ten centimeters above ground), ready to shoot rows of jars and cough out radioactive clouds. She, my K bride, wearing a dress of graphite that leaves her knees uncovered, has her core filled with fuel, and she can't wait to burn it. Ours is a passionate relationship.

Yes, I'm drunk, and full of metastases of impossible, of radioactive cheetah stains making me run breathlessly to overcome my thoughts; impossible, them too, by now. I don't want to listen to them, I cannot.

I drink on them, drown them.

All this bullshit comes from the bottle, that much is clear… I'm sucking bullshit from the glass and I spit it out, just as it is, on these pages I found by chance.

Ozram comes by once a week for a Nazi search, equipped with trash bags, to throw away anything that hurts me. *That mustachioed mule…* So I have bottles hidden everywhere: drawers, cabinets, underwear, cardboard boxes over cupboards—where I fished out this now-dead journal, together with the worst autumn I could meet: fallen leaves, scattered, their corners dry and curled, and her printed on them, hair of grain and a dead smile—Lada's old photos: her first day at school, and then at the swimming pool, her with the red suit on and a couple of tangerines just jutting out. *But not that pool…*

I no longer remember what I wrote in here many years ago. And neither do I wish to re-read, reminisce. *Comfortably Numb*, Pink Floyd, 1979 (I'm becoming better than Ozram with music)…that should be today's soundtrack.

Boom! Explosion. Atomic spleen. Is it really over?

Everything, they say, is burnt and gone, an old toxic dream now drifting in the air, legs running here and there, over the skies of Eastern Europe, with the tip of its nose on the Yankee coasts (yes, it will reach them). Boni…sniff the air and hope to breathe in her ashes, something of her. This is me.

And all those people around her? The same people decimated by our Karakurts and who, on that night, must have naively admired the spectacle of the light shining over the reactor. *An out-of-time atomic sunrise.*

I need a double coffee before I continue to scribble on these blank sheets. I'll try again in a few hours, less drunk than now; maybe.

Boom! Explosion. The images, the aftermath. A surreal march of scores of buses, stuffed with evacuees, their mouths open, moving souls in a hurry...now parked in the forbidden area in a sort of dead zone. A Blue Bus to the tenth power has turned its engines back on, the one The Doors sang about twenty years ago, the one carrying American soldiers, evacuees from their lives (they, too) to training bases for The Vietnam War. Sparks and napalm, choppers whipping the forest and then (just today), with red stars painted on their tails, dropping thousands of tons of boron, dolomite, clay on the reactor, to put out the fire. *This is the End...*

I feel better, but not so much. I look in the mirror and I'm there...good, but I cannot see my living room, like a landfill, behind me. The plant appears, its guts ripped open, and all around an anthill of liquidators, miners, zombies at work. Everything is in black and white, painted in graphite, but then from the ruins I see a colored butterfly soar, a body made of specks of dust, with Boni's drawings on its wings. A patchwork of men and women, an apocalyptic orgy of medals on raw skin and lacking (or burst) hearts. *Am I still drunk?*

A cold shower—that's what I need.

I've cut out a newspaper article about the April 27 evacuation; I want to glue it below here. If only I could find some glue, or anything else, in this house...

Warning, warning: Trusty Comrades, the communal council of representatives informs us that, following an accident at the electronuclear Chernobyl plant in the city of Prip'jat, the quantity of radiation in the air has increased beyond acceptable standards. Thanks to the Communist Party and the Soviet police force, the necessary emergency measures are underway. So as to ensure the complete safety of the population, especially our children, it is necessary to temporarily evacuate citizens from the Kiev area. Consequently, every flat will be cleared, and today, April 27, from 14:00, autobuses will be made available for the evacuation by the police and local representatives of the Party. You are urged to bring with you: identity documents, as strictly necessary, and food for the first day. Thanks to our State institutions, lists of workers will be compiled to ensure the normal functioning of the city. All flats, during the evacuations, will be monitored by police agents. Comrades, as you temporarily clear your homes, please, don't forget to close all windows, turn off all electrical and gas systems, and close all faucets. Please, remain calm, organized, and orderly during this temporary evacuation.

A recipe for fear, dressed in camo suit, that can do nothing at all against leukemia, thyroid cancer, and everything brooding within those people, like a green lizard camouflaged among their DNA helices, ready to leap, launched by its tail, and bite with its amaranth teeth. The fearful voices of people, an imaginary William Blake suddenly turning toward his wife, there on the window seat of the jammed blue bus, his hands on his face, screaming to her with doomsday urgency: *Stay, Kate! Keep just as you are—I will draw your portrait—for you have ever been an angel to me.*

Photographs of newborn ghosts. I can't go on.

I keep drinking, I haven't stopped since I resumed wasting ink on this… I'm doing my worst, yet I can't catch the tail of that damned ape wedged in my head…that keeps shrieking, thrumming anguish and molding, with the pellets of its feces, the same mental picture: Boni, melted in the underground uterus of that cursed plutonium cathedral. A lifeless puddle, with a leather lace inside, an aquamarine hanging from it—surely fake.

They're knocking at the door. I'll have to open it, before Ozram begins shouldering it. In my heart, I hope it's Violetta instead, a lace tight around her arm and eyes of misery: she would dance again for me, for a green or blue bill, narcotizing it all.

Knocking again, *that mustachioed mule...*

JUNE 16, 1986
KIEV

I left Moscow a week ago, and I haven't had a drink since.

I'm back in Kiev—not at the Radisson Blu this time, and not at that weird clinic. Mine is a crazy suicide mission, but I have nothing to lose now. I have to know what happened to Boni, to crush my obsession for the girl from Kiev once and for all. I'm an old wreck, and even Ozram—my good guardian devil—has dumped me; but I have a plan.

No news from the plant, they pretend they don't even know me. No surprise there: many years have passed, and the plutonium cathedral still stands—though marred by the explosion—with three reactors operational (and two more under construction, for now at least). The Hole is just an old memory, and they probably cleared everything out, down there, from the Safe Zone to the old underground reactor—the one that never worked. No trace of Adrianov the-Lanky, the Hole director; it seems he never existed. Skinny as he was back then, he probably just consumed himself. Who knows where they sent his heap of bones?

All the scientific staff has vanished, and I think I know how all the witnesses of the ruinous Prometheus Project ended up. The last thing before their eyes must have been Rostok's glass eye. Today, General Semerov should be around ninety-five years old; he surely was a tough guy, Soviet fiber, but I don't think he could still be on his feet. At that age, surviving the reconditioning camps is really too hard. Kireyev was swallowed by the KGB black hole, no doubt, and probably nobody ever heard from him again. He must be dreaming about his dacha in a nameless pit in the dirt.

So, at the end of the day, I'm probably the last link to that strange story, unless...Boni survived. *Possible?*

Unless they got rid of her years ago, in the Safe Zone. It could be the case (*but why keep her in a cell for so long?* She certainly wasn't the wreck of some crashed spaceship, the precious source of alien technology). Surely, the explosion of Reactor 4 couldn't damage the Hole—or what was left of the underground facility.

And the high radiation level now spreading around the plant caused by the disaster wouldn't have been an issue for a creature expressly modeled to survive (and fight) in such an extreme habitat: the now notorious Exclusion Zone—vacated and inaccessible—that can either kill you on the spot, or eventually. With patience, and little mercy.

Of course, it's my obsession that coaxes me toward the impossible, just as it managed to bring me here—with nothing but the suit I'm wearing and four suitcases full of scientific tools and instruments. I took what I needed from my Lomonosov lab…they must already be looking for me, but I believe I have a lead of several days.

The days I need.

It's raining, outside. Radioactive contamination is coming down vertically now, too, beside running horizontally from one side of the planet to the other. *Bad rain.*

We're a hundred kilometers from the plant, and a hungry wind has been blowing for days. Everything interlocks, sometimes. Like DNA helices. Things fit together.

In this flat (rented thanks to the good graces of Rasim, one of my few contacts in Kiev) I feel safe. One bedroom, a small living room, bathroom, kitchen, and a roomy storage closet where I've stored my special contraptions. I know, it's sheer madness. *A seventy-year-old Prometheus*… sounds ludicrous, and probably is. I'll croak, but it will be worth it.

No, I'm not drunk—not right now—and I did my home-work sober: *I have a chance,* after all; technology has come a long way, since those times in the Bunker. Now, I don't need assistance or bulky machines to manage a self-treatment. And then again, I certainly don't need to undergo a complete mutation, not even mid-tier…at my age, I could never endure all the necessary steps.

Achieving Level 2 will be more than enough for what I have to do: to go into the Exclusion Zone without getting killed; thoroughly scout out the area (it will take several days); and find Boni, if I'm lucky. If she managed to get out of the Hole, taking advantage of the security system breakdown after the reactor explosion, she must have stayed close to the optimal environment she was forged for. Where she's safe.

She won't get far.

Another of the weird coincidences in this story: the battlefield we pictured for our chosen ones now exists, right there at Chernobyl—though we pictured it differently, and much bigger.

If she's still a prisoner, trying to break into the plant facility—to reach the Hole and the Safe Zone—it's not an option; surveillance is tight, and getting in after the disaster is virtually impossible...even though, a few days from now, I'll be able to rely on a good amount of K liquid plutonium in my DNA, and on a new atomic youth—its long-term effects on my body unforeseeable. The body of an old drunk like me, not exactly ideal.

Third hypothesis—the one I don't even want to consider—is that the girl from Kiev was done in a long time ago... If that's the case, then all this plotting and preparation is for a ghost hunt. It won't be the first time, after all. By now, I'm an expert on ghosts... I'm more in touch with them than with the living.

So, considering all the possible scenarios, I became convinced that *I have a chance*, and I'm holding on to that. What may seem absurd to some is not for others— who've already reached a certain point in their lives. There are moments, short and steep, where your bush is full of blackberries, big and ripe, black and red, all within reach. Handfuls of things to grasp even with your eyes closed. Some other times, times with white hair and a lazy bladder, you must be patient, search among the branches, shake them, scratch your face and arms, climb, crawl into the bush even if you didn't see anything good from outside. Opportunities become small, almost invisible, and numbered like the deluxe edition of a good novel.

It keeps raining. My bones burn, and while today's third drip-feed does its job in my arm—the drops look almost solid—I look at the bend of the river through the window specked by carabines of dark rain, as it keeps pushing water toward its natural destination, never stopping. The Dnepr is as strong and rich today as it must have been many other times, a hundred years ago, even two hundred.

It doesn't get old. It cannot die. That only happens to men.

JUNE 18, 1986
KIEV

Three more days and I'll go looking for Boni.

The self-treatment appears to be proceeding well; my plutonium cocktails have already brought me to Level 1. A hundred rubles—slipped into the pocket of the shortnecked man at the lab on Mykylskyi corner—were enough to get all the papers I needed, and to shut his mouth. Vodka night for him, I'll bet, but not for me this time. Not until my mutation is complete and I go exploring in the Exclusion Zone. *Where are you, Boni?*

This is my tenth day of the simplified procedure, here in Kiev; I'm forcing the pace, but I can't wait to leave for Chernobyl. Intramuscular injections for radioactive neutron-capture hydrolase have worked well in the place of direct irradiation, and drip-feeds for K liquid plutonium, Rad 51 proteins, inhibitors, enzymes and recombiners have proved an excellent alternative to full pool immersions. The Geiger counter and the analysis reports I've just collected do justice to my calculations. My gene pool is about to face the first spike in the atomic quality leap. I won't be able to evolve like the chosen ones, and tissue regeneration traits will stay dormant, or undergo imperceptible alterations; but that will be enough to move at ease across the radioactive inferno waiting for me. For a few days, at least.

I feel good, now, though the first few days in gave me nausea, fever, sharp bone pains, and some sight disorders, forcing me to stay shut in this small flat. Divided from a world in upheaval, in my makeshift genetic engineering lab.

Each time I absentmindedly open the fridge, I open my eyes wide: so much stuff in there—convex tubes, glowing containers, and racks of test tubes with colored caps—and so little to satisfy a hungry stomach, that I wonder if I've gone completely mad.

What am I doing? Then, the answer comes straight like an arrow at my back, straightening me up. *Boni, it's all for her.* The half-kilo blackberry hiding deep in the bush, the one nobody saw; that nobody even suspects.

Today, I went out for the second time since arriving in the city, to pick up the reports and restock on food, syringes, tubes, and other rather common materials required to carry out the procedure. In my four suitcases—by now half-empty—I already had all the non-conventional medical ammo; you certainly can't buy those at the drugstore.

I used the opportunity for a walk along the river. The atmosphere here in Kiev is really strange, some days after the reactor explosion. Shop shelves are almost empty, people are shut in their houses, and the wind runs through spaces more freely than usual, meeting few obstacles...but then, from the throats of stately buildings, little human files pop out, swaying—heads big and small, like the bodies attached to them—in a funeral-like gait. Parents leading their children to the family doctor, or golden-handed specialists, to try and comprehend the effects of the radioactive cloud, snarling loud here, only a hundred kilometers from its source. They've read so many contradictory things, they're disoriented.

A few years from now, the cancer registries of every city will need new archives for all the clinical documentation spawned by the disaster. Legions of incoming terminal patients, their faces gray with fear and their right arms busy in an ongoing, steady sign of the cross...even the most communist, or those holding dolls with singed hair in their small arms. Today, they all look perfectly healthy, they cannot feel that invisible X—already branded between their shoulder blades. It doesn't burn, not yet.

A timer, that's what you hear along the street, in this too-silent city…something ticking time away, with deadline urgency, like the accelerating beeps of a bomb already primed.

And yet, you don't notice a real panic spreading across the city. *Is that the narcotic effect of incredulity?* As far as I can tell, not everybody believes that the Green Apocalypse is coming (though a miniature one). They're vaccinated by propaganda rubbish, and they suspect it's a trick to dispossess people of large areas and brand-new cities, like Pripyat, to military ends and to the bureaucrats' shadowy interests. *Maybe they found oil down there?*

An elderly woman sitting in front of her produce shop— her wide printed dress too cheerful against the apocalyptic gray painted everywhere—stood and grabbed my arm, saying with conviction: *Don't listen to those radiation stories. Look at these potatoes, how clean they are…*

She was selling death, and she ate it with her family without even knowing.

JUNE 19, 1986
KIEV

It finally stopped raining.

I undressed and took my time looking at myself in the mirror. My skin is beginning to show pigmentation changes: the light blue of the chosen ones, slightly perceptible. When I'm be ready to go out, to move toward the Exclusion Zone, it will be still unnoticeable.

My muscles feel more vigorous, and I'm almost sure I'm at least five centimeters taller. But I have no way of measuring that here. This was never reported in the other subjects, not even at higher mutation levels than mine, but it may be a consequence of my age. *I got shorter: am I now returning to what I used to be?* How many other things should I expect?

It's all so absurd… I lost my will to live a long time ago, and that's exactly why I decided to devote everything I have left to an impossible adventure. A beautiful suicide, ultimately. *Because I well* *know, inside of me, that I'll never find the girl from Kiev...*but trying is more important than succeeding.

But, at the same time, I'm slowly returning to the threshold of my youth, and I feel the ancient sensations awakening, and something new, too—in my head, I hear Janis Joplin singing—and I'm sure I can perceive Lada, her almond scent... It's as though she were still leaning on my shoulder, a yellow day more than forty years ago...and I'm singing her a song from the future, *One Night Stand*, to make her fall asleep.

And then, like the river outside, unmoving between its shores, other emotions quickly flow in three dimensions, warm amniotic waters. Tides. Just as I'm writing this, another one comes, through the lines. The old house where I grew up, on one of the Vicebsk humps, the garden and the rows of ants, the blue bathroom, almost a burrow, the window squeezing the belly of the Daugava—another river, water again coming and going—Chagall lithographies, my father cleaning his pistol, tiny springs on the bed. *Be careful, Pavel, don't touch anything!* The scent of draniki emanating from the kitchen, *mushroom and bacon, just as I like them*, breakfast ready on the table, my mother's smile, pulled by hair lacquer, a black eye and her sadness always dying soon.

Five hundred kilometers from here, four hundred from Chernobyl, and from Boni.

JUNE 20, 1986
KIEV

I've just bought a red 1973 Lada 1200, and filled her up.

Tomorrow, that car will take me to the Exclusion Zone: it's all set. My treatment is complete, everything going according to plan, but my sight has significantly worsened. I should change my glasses, but there's no time. I didn't expect that such an incomplete mutation level could lead to side effects like these; it never happened with other Level 1 subjects at the Balapan Bunker.

My other senses feel brand new, as though I were twenty. I feel strong, and I'm beginning to think of Boni in a different way. She was a Muse, a daughter, a fleshless and bloodless obsession. It's different now, and I feel like a fool. *A companion? My petite girl from Kiev?* It could never work, though we almost belong to the same species now; I've always been something different for her, and when she hugged me in her cell, the last time I saw her— *take me away from here*—she was hugging a father, a friend, a sexless body, or simply someone who might help her. Despair, of course. Perhaps, she simply hated me, and still does, for what I turned her into: a prisoner of her own plutonium blood, of a cell upholstered in color nightmares.

But these inner drives, this mocking kaleidoscope through which I now look at Boni as she dances and capsizes, different, more womanlike, *woman only*—they've brought other things with them. Things from a much more recent past. Bottles. Vodka. Alcohol. Once again, I have an empty glass at hand as I write and rant.

Youth found again, like an old photograph in a magic box, sucking you back to where you were, as you were... or simple, sad madness?

There's no cure or treatment for loneliness.

Luckily, they knock at the door. I already know who it is.

I was waiting for him, old Rasim, same old hair standing on end.

Professor Todorov, I'm so glad! Good to see you again out of there...

Last time I'd spoken to him on the phone (he was helping me to find this place to stay), I'd asked him to drop by. *I have a surprise for you, something special...*

We had a drink together. He talked at length about his daughter Amina in the present tense, as though she were still alive. He isn't crazy, despite his stay in the clinic some years ago—the same could be said about me.

Loneliness is witchcraft: it molds things, polishes them. It makes them so real that you have to believe in them. And so, I discovered many things about that kid, taken from a garden by night; as though a shred of time—when she was between fifteen and seventeen years old—had frozen solid inside my friend's mind, always day-fresh. A powerful delusion, mescaline hypnotism allowing him tell, with remarkable vividness, of the early-June ball at the church in Rudko, their village. Amina's orange dress, the music, long tables lined with people and fragrant tomatoes, bare feet at dusk, and a fat moon behind the hill...where he'd caught his daughter with a curly-haired boy. *I chased him across the town. You should have seen it!*

As he spoke, he ran his fingers through his reddish beard, where more words seemed to be hiding—anecdotes, grains of that girl to be put back together, like beads on a string.

I let him vent; during those months at the clinic I learned to know that man, and now I could see he needed just that: to talk a little bit of his days of tin. Then, a sort of autopilot would bring him back to the "here and now," leaving Amina aside.

Time to show him my surprise. I got up, reached into the storage closet, and grabbed the shoe box where I'd hidden my "gift."

He waited for me on the couch, his mouth open, eyes flitting up and down, lively and smiling eyes. *I wasn't expecting... Come on, let me see.*

When he saw what it was—below that cardboard lid— he raised his gaze to me, his expression changing as he brought his large hands to cover his face. Then, he reappeared; different, older, tears in his eyes. *My friend*...he said, twice, squeezing his fists and looking up to where he thought his daughter was—*heaven*?

He grasped that grim item, ran his fingers over it, then put it back, closed the box, stood and moved his hand in a strange gesture. Like a hatchet splitting the air. Like saying: *Back to my days of tin, now, or whatever else.*

I had just given him Konstantin's visor—such was my surprise.

That night at the farmhouse, I took it from the floor littered with glass, blood, brains. After planting a bullet in my chosen one's mouth, the device had snapped away from his face. I slipped it under my coat and then, lying on the ground, I raised my hands as the raging squad of cleaners broke in.

Rasim immediately understood what it was; and when he brushed it—the tip of his index finger circling its closed, dead lens—he must have thought that gear, with the bad soul behind it, had been the last thing framing his daughter alive.

Now that he owns the head of his monster, I hope my friend's ghosts will vanish, together with the nights which keep tormenting him with relentless gunshots; each time, the clock marks the hour Amina was dragged away.

Rain again; it resumed immediately after Rasim left, his precious box under his arm, after loitering for a while near my new car, parked in front. He didn't ask me about that story, about Karakurt, odd; he immediately went back to talking about his daughter in the present tense, about his wife, about Bosnian dishes I should taste—*Hana has golden hands for certain things*—making me promise I'll visit him, someday, in Rudko.

Someday… I don't think I have many days left.

He didn't even notice the strange color of my skin, or the fact that I look so young for my age. Perhaps, the strength of my handshake surprised him, when I welcomed him— he started…but that may have been just be my impression. Nothing more. I believe old Rasim's sight isn't so good. It took him a couple of seconds to even recognize the visor.

My own eyes are struggling ever more, especially during the day. I have to keep the windows open and the lights off. And now, after my friend's visit, my eyes burn.

But enough with the writing for today. Forever, maybe—should I actually find Boni.

This journal—what it has become, over time, changing along with me and all the world around us—is nothing more now than an appendix of the girl from Kiev, a way to find her, not to forget.

Look Homeward, Angel, Wolfe wrote.

Not to Be Afraid

June, 30 1986
Černobyl' – Exclusion Zone
Red Forest

I found her. I walked for a week, but I finally found her, here in the Red Forest, inside the Exclusion Zone ring, a few kilometers north of the plant. Four hundred hectares soaked with gamma rays, dead dark trunks, apocalyptic burnt fences jutting from a floor of brick-colored pine needles. Still screaming softwoods, twisted like spineless odalisques with blackened ankles. A dance that stopped mid-air, devoid of skin, and organs kept together by the boiling glue of the fallout.

She was right here; among trees and plants splattered in bright Modigliani red—the painted wall of a brothel crowded with hearts and fossil chests—which no longer know how to decompose. Rusty ghosts holding tight to one another, like fifteen-meter-high wooden bars of a huge prison, behind which packs of wild, animal eyes pop up, like yellow and white bunches of grapes.

She was hiding; far from the yellow signs that cordoned off the area, from the checkpoints watched by soldiers, their camo suits riddled with invisible holes—of bullets that don't hurt yet—and a double rosary of concentric circles at their neck. Far from the map they keep looking at, while praying to be relieved soon. The map marking the borders between the fast-death zone—half an hour—and the patient one. The sponge. The one that can wait, before sticking her bony black hands into your mouth to make your tongue bitter, like the aquifers beneath us.

She was like a song in the distance, driving you with its unending, bullheaded loop. It seemed to whisper strange, dark verses, tied around an obsessive drumming rhythm. '*Follow your crazy diamond, believe to yourself. Come on, seer of visions, entrust to your flesh compass. Go North of the prison of your senses, and let your demon shine.*'

That's how I found her.

I walked for a week, and then Boni appeared behind the still-standing corpse of a Scottish pine, its bark all scraped away. Who knows how long she'd been following me, peeking, thinking about what to do?

She'd escaped the Hole. She was still alive. I was right.

I stopped, waited until it was she who approached me. *Did she want to kill me or take me to her shelter?* Did she have a lair?

Even from that distance—about twenty meters—I noticed immediately that her black eyes were gone…those almonds that would stare at me every day from these pages, attached to the old photo that always separates the before and the after of this journal: the point I reached; the point from where I resumed.

That intermittent red light under her forehead…naturally, they'd grafted a visor to her, and now she was looking at me through the electric signals of a machine.

She came closer, taking small steps, stopping here and there for a few seconds, and tilting her head sideways, as if to better frame me in her optic gear—much like Konstantin's, which ended up in a shoe box.

Once she was near—her face blue and her naked arms a bright cobalt—and I felt her quick breath blowing, she slowly raised her arms to my face. I grabbed her wrists, stopping her, making her bite her lips. I didn't know what to expect...but I was aware I had something delicious in my skull for her, something warm. But then, I let her do it—did it matter? Death was an option in my plan.

If she decided to smash my head and eat my memories, I would stay with her forever, inside my girl from Kiev. No longer alone, I could take off my black coat at last, one way or another.

With her freed hands—cold as snow—she began brushing my face, lingering around my closed eyes, then pressing an index finger against my lips. Not a word, besides her breath coming closer and closer, moving toward my neck. She was smelling me—as you'd smell a prey to consider its edibility. *Had she recognized me?*

Suddenly, she shoved me down, my back to the ground, and she straddled me. I opened my eyes, just in time to see her animating those lips that looked as if they were sealed, covered in their strange glowing-green hoarfrost.

Take me away from here. The same words of many years ago, but in a more decisive tone. I hadn't vanished from her memory. She didn't hate me for what I'd done to her, and for leaving her behind in that cell, among her obscure drawings that I could never entirely comprehend.

Her way of communicating?

In that moment, I remembered that odd sketch in her cell, noticed many years before: a forest splattered in red, an angel on the ground and a blue-skinned woman straddling him.

Of course, the two of us, right now...

It must be. Enough with the weird, absurd coincidences that I've tried to ignore, black holes only leading me to a bottle after another—as though alcohol could melt away things beyond understanding.

Finally, Boni grinned; I wasn't her prey, not at all. *Take me away from here*, again, squeezing my shoulders, shaking me. Then she tilted her head, leaning toward me, letting me see her mouth—back to orange, as by magic— coming down on mine.

It happened fast. A gunshot made my ears ring. Immediately, Boni straightened her back, springing as though someone had stuck a high-voltage cable up her spine. She tried to leverage herself to her feet pushing on my chest with her hands. Another shot, and she collapsed upon me, motionless. Her blood—blue, so dark and cold— cooled my chest and spread, thick, across the pine needles.

Yells in the distance, then closer. *That voice...*

Two shapes came out of nothingness. I could see no details in the poor light. I only saw two faces above me, framed by consumed treetops. They wore masks that warped their harsh features. It was sunset and my eyes hadn't been working well for a while...and maybe shock made things worse.

Was Boni dead?

I felt their arms taking her weight away from me, putting me back on my feet, and then strongly holding me. When my sight came back to show me things more clearly, I saw...and understood. Holding my arms behind my back, a sturdy man forced me to kneel on the ground. The other one, standing beside Boni's body—her chest still showing signs of life, quickly heaving—I knew him well. It was old Rasim: his hair standing on end and his build gave him away despite the gas mask covering part of his face. He carried a shotgun, an odd sneer on his face. He turned to look at me for a second, spat out a few words, then he leveled the barrel of his weapon, placing it against Boni's visor. *Damn monsters!* he screamed before squeezing the trigger. Once, twice. Then he reloaded and kept shooting the lifeless body.

I looked at the sky, but no bird—nothing, in fact— was escaping, flying away from that hell of blasts and blasphemies.

The forest was dead, like the girl from Kiev.

After venting, Rasim approached me and gestured to the man holding me. I felt a blow to my head, then I remember nothing else.

Clearly, they had followed me for days. That's why Rasim was so interested in my car. They were patient, waiting for the right moment. Maybe, the old madman had noticed my light-bluish skin, as well as other signs of mutation after all—changes I'd thought imperceptible. But of course, suspicion dawned when I gave him

Konstantin's visor. *How could I have it, without having had some role in that story of monsters?*

The brawny man who held me had to be Heldar, Amina's older brother. Rasim had told me about him at the clinic. He could be nobody else. Things come full circle for real this time—for them, too. They took their revenge knowing that to enter the Exclusion Zone was suicide, despite their gas masks and any protection gear they might use. They would die atrociously, they knew that, but they did it without a second thought.

I was a fool. I led the hunt to my Muse, to my new Eve.

But I have something left, to keep living for…

When I woke up, in the middle of the night, I found myself in this forest—turned from red into black—together with Boni's dead body. They'd laid her down beside me. We looked like newlyweds in death.

They spared my life, sure, but not out of mercy…just to make me pay in the worst possible way. Rasim well knows that remaining, with the burden of memory and pain, is worse than going, saying goodbye this so-temporary chunk of universe. He knows it well—since it's the reason he went mad. And he, too, is going to go before me, unless I off myself before.

But I have something left, to keep living for. *Her,* still, in spite of everything. I buried her body under a large fir— its head cut off by the fire—and I set a stone to mark the spot. I'm going to put this journal down there, too; it will stay with her, because it's useless to me now. I will graft her visor to myself before I go blind, and I'll see through her final eyes.

I'll watch over Boni for all the time I have left. In a few years, they'll come here, to the Red Forest to check radiation levels, collect ground samples and who knows what else; I won't allow them to find her, to take her away to a lab and slice her up and study her.

I won't allow that. I'll be the keeper of this grave, I'll speak to her, I'll tell her not to be afraid, I will sing her all the songs I remember.

Multiple Bram Stoker Award Winner

Alessandro Manzetti

The Keeper of Chernobyl

About the Author

Alessandro Manzetti (Rome, Italy) is a three-time Bram Stoker Award-winning author (an fourteen times nominated), editor, and scriptwriter of horror fiction and dark poetry whose work has been published extensively in Italian and English, including novels, short and long fiction, poetry, essays, and collections. English publications include his novels *Naraka—The Ultimate Human Breeding* and *Shanti: The Sadist Heaven*, the collections *The Radioactive Bride*, *The Garden of Delight*, the guide *Exquisite Horror: Essential Guide to the Best 150 Books*, the graphic novels (with Stefano Cardoselli) *Calcutta Horror, The Inhabitant of the Lake* and *Kraken Inferno*, and the poetry collections *Kubrick Rhapsody* (with Karen Runge), *Dancing with Maria's Ghosts, Whitechapel Rhapsody, No Mercy, Eden Underground, The Place of Broken Things* (with Linda D. Addison), *War* (with Marge Simon) *Sacrificial Nights* (with Bruce Boston) and *Venus Intervention* (with Corrine de Winter). He edited the anthologies *The Beauty of Death, The Beauty of Death Vol. 2 —Death by Water* (with Jodi Renee Lester) and *Monsters of Any Kind* (with Daniele Bonfanti).

His stories and poems have appeared in Italian, USA, UK, Australian, Canadian, Russian and Polish magazines such as Weird Tales Magazine, Dark Moon Digest, Splatterpunk Zine, Disturbed Digest, Space and Time Magazine, Darker Magazine, The Horror Zine, Dark Moon Digest, Illumen, Devolution Z, Hinnom, Recompose, Polu Texni, Nothing's Sacred, Okolica Strachu, and anthologies such as *The Best Horror of the Year* Vol. 13, *Classic Monsters Unleashed, Splatterpunk Forever, Best Hardcore Horror of the Year* Vol. 2, 4, 5, 6, *The Big Book of Blasphemy, Midnight Under the Big Top*, Rhysling Anthologies, HWA Poetry Showcase Vol. 3, 4, 9, *Shakespeare Unleashed, World of Light and Darkness, One of Us, Hybrid: Misfits, Monsters and Other Phenomena*, and many others. He has won the SFPA Elgin Award, and has been nominated (besides the Bram Stoker Awards) also for the Splatterpunk Awards, This Is Horror Awards, Rhysling Awards. Website: **www.battiago.com**

MONSTERS

Available Books in English

STRANGE TALES OF TERROR
Edited by Eugene Johnson
Anthology – Paperback Edition
December 2022

KUBRICK RHAPSODY
by Alessandro Manzetti and Karen Runge
Poetry Collection – Paperback Edition
December 2022

THE ANA-LOG AND OTHER ANOMALIES
by Michael Gray Baughan
Fiction Collection – Paperback Edition
November 2022

MOBIUS LYRICS
by Angela Yuriko Smith & Maxwell I. Gold
Poetry Collection– Paperback Edition
October 2022

MOBIUS LYRICS
by Angela Yuriko Smith & Maxwell I. Gold
Poetry Collection– Paperback Edition
October 2022

THIS ATTRACTION NOW COMING TILL LATE
by Kyla Lee Ward
Collection– Paperback Edition
September 2022

KRAKEN INFERNO
by Alessandro Manzetti and Stefano Cardoselli
Graphic Novel – Paperback Edition
April 2022

DANCING WITH MARIA'S GHOST
by Alessandro Manzetti i
Poetry Collection– Paperback Edition
December 2021

THE INHABITANT OF THE LAKE
by Alessandro Manzetti and Stefano Cardoselli
Graphic Novel – Paperback Edition
December 2021

BLACK MOUNTAIN
by Simon Bestwick
Novel – Paperback and eBook Edition
November 2021

APACHE WITCH
by Joe R. Lansdale
Poetry Collection – Hardcover Edition
September 2021

THE FEVERISH STARS
by John Shirley
Collection – Paperback and eBook Edition
March 2021

HER LIFE MATTERS
by Alessandro Manzetti and Stefano Cardoselli
Graphic Novel – Paperback Edition
December 2020

UMBRIA
by Santiago Eximeno
Collection – Paperback and eBook Edition
December 2020

LOST TRIBE
by Gene O'Neill
Novel – Paperback and eBook Edition
October 2020

SHILOH
by Philip Fracassi
Novella – Paperback and eBook Edition
October 2020

WHITECHAPEL RHAPSODY
by Alessandro Manzetti
Poetry Collection – Paperback and eBook Edition
October 2020

RED DENNIS
by Eric Shapiro
Novel – Paperback and eBook Edition
March 2020

THE DEMETER DIARIES
by Marge Simon and Bryan D. Dietrich
Prose/Poetry Collection – Paperback and eBook Edition
October 2019

THE MAN WHO ESCAPED THIS STORY AND OTHER STORIES
by Cody Goodfellow
Collection – Paperback and eBook Edition
September 2019

CROTA
by Owl Goingback
Novel – Hardcover, Paperback and eBook Edition
July 2019

DARK CARNIVAL
by Joanna Parypinski
Novel – Paperback and eBook Edition
June 2019

CALCUTTA HORROR
by Alessandro Manzetti & Stefano Cardoselli
Graphic Novel – Paperback and eBook Edition
May 2019

COYOTE RAGE
by Owl Goingback
Novel – Paperback and eBook Edition
February 2019

APARTMENT SEVEN
by Greg F. Gifune
Novella – Paperback and eBook Edition
Juanuary 2019

FEARFUL SYMMETRIES
by Thomas F. Monteleone
Collection – Paperback and eBook Edition
January 2019

DARK MARY
by Paolo Di Orazio
Novel – Paperback and eBook Edition
December 2018

TRIBAL SCREAMS
by Owl Goingback
Collection – Paperback and eBook Edition
October 2018

MONSTERS OF ANY KIND
Edited by Alessandro Manzetti & Daniele Bonfanti
Stories by: David J. Schow, Edward Lee,
Jonathan Maberry, Ramsey Campbell,
Lucy Taylor, Cody Goodfellow and many others
Anthology – Paperback and eBook Edition
September 2018

ARTIFACTS
by Bruce Boston
Poetry Collection– Paperback and eBook Edition
July 2018

KNOWING WHEN TO DIE
by Mort Castle
Collection– Paperback and eBook Edition
June 2018

NARAKA
by Alessandro Manzetti
Novel– Paperback and eBook Edition
May 2018

A WINTER SLEEP
by Greg F. Gifune
Novel– Paperback and eBook Edition
April 2018

SPREE AND OTHER STORIES
by Lucy Taylor
Collection – Paperback and eBook Edition
February 20

THE LIVING AND THE DEAD
by Greg F. Gifune
Novel – Paperback and eBook Edition
December 2017

TALKING IN THE DARK
by Dennis Etchison
Collection – eBook Edition
December 2017

THE BEAUTY OF DEATH 2 – DEATH BY WATER
edited by Alessandro Manzetti & Jodi Renee Lester
Anthology – Paperback and eBook Edition
November 2017

DREAMS THE RAGMAN
by Greg F. Gifune
Novella – Paperback and eBook Edition
November 2017

CHILDREN OF NO ONE
by Nicole Cushing
Novella – Paperback and eBook Edition
October 2017

THE RAIN DANCERS
by Greg F. Gifune
Novella – Paperback and eBook Edition
September 2017

THE WISH MECHANICS
by Daniel Braum
Collection – Paperback and eBook Edition
July 2017

THE ONE THAT COMES BEFORE
by Livia Llewellyn
Novella – Paperback and eBook Edition
May 2017

SELECTED STORIES
by Nate Southard
Collection – Paperback and eBook Edition
March 2017

THE CARP-FACED BOY AND OTHER TALES
by Thersa Matsuura
Collection – Paperback and eBook Edition
February 2017

DOCTOR BRITE
by Poppy Z. Brite
Collection – eBook Edition
December 2016

ALL AMERICAN HORROR OF THE 21ST CENTURY: THE FIRST DECADE
edited by Mort Castle
Anthology – Paperback and eBook Edition
November 2016

BENEATH THE NIGHT
by Greg Gifune
Novel – Paperback and eBook Edition
October 2016

WHAT WE FOUND IN THE WOODS
by Shane McKenzie
Collection – eBook Edition
September 2016

THE HORROR SHOW
by Poppy Z. Brite
Collection – eBook Edition
August 2016

THE BEAUTY OF DEATH VOL. 1
Edited by Alessandro Manzetti
Anthology – eBook Edition
July 2016

SELECTED STORIES
by Edward Lee
Collection – eBook Edition
July 2016

USED STORIES
by Poppy Z. Brite
Collection – eBook Edition
June 2016
THE USHERS
by Edward Lee
Collection – eBook Edition
May 2016

THE CRYSTAL EMPIRE
by Poppy Z. Brite
Novella – eBook Edition
April 2016

SONGS FOR THE LOST
by Alexander Zelenyj
Collection – eBook Edition
April 2016

SELECTED STORIES
by Poppy Z. Brite
Collection – eBook Edition
February 2016

THE HITCHHIKING EFFECT
by Gene O'Neill
Collection – eBook Edition
February 2016

INDEPENDENT LEGIONS PUBLISHING
Via Virgilio, 10 – TRIESTE (ITALY)
+39 040 9776602
www.independentlegions.com
independent.legions@aol.com

www.ingramcontent.com/pod-product-compliance
Lightning Source LLC
LaVergne TN
LVHW091056150826
845673LV00002B/596

* 9 7 9 1 2 8 0 7 1 3 6 4 3 *